FICTION

INQUIRIES & ADVERTISING

Address: Suite 22, 509 Commissioners Road West, London, Ontario, N6J 1Y5

Advertising: Email info@mysterymagazine.ca

Editor: Kerry Carter **Publisher:** Chuck Carter **Cover Artist:** Robin Grenville Evans

Submissions: https://mysterymagazine.ca/submit.asp

MILLER AND BELL

Victor Kreuiter

Dutch Miller listened for as long as he could stomach it. There were three of them sitting in Deena Hoke's cramped living room, listening to her drone on and on. Miller had been lured with the story of fast work and a big take. Deena'd been hyping the thing for over an hour and the longer she went on the less likely it sounded. Miller didn't know the other two guys, was unfamiliar with the city where it would happen and was unsure about the target. As she prattled on about how easy and rewarding it would be he made up his mind: it was a wild goose chase.

He stood up and stretched, his move to show he was going to leave. She looked at him, scowled, and pointed a finger.

"Sit down, Dutch. Now."

He didn't sit down. He frowned, stared at her, walked to Deena, hung his head—wanting to appear contrite—and said "Sorry Deena. I'm out." He didn't want to make a scene, didn't want any drama, but was no longer interested. Decision final.

He hadn't seen Deena Hoke in years and hadn't ever really known her well. He looked into her eyes, shrugged out an apology, and was turning toward the door when she grabbed his arm. "You're not leaving," she said. She leaned closer until they were face to face. "Nobody's quitting. Not now, not after you've heard the plan." Was it a threat? It took him a second to realize she'd threatened him. He wondered how Deena Hoke had convinced herself she had the stones to do that.

And she'd touched him. Dutch Miller did not like being touched.

He punched her. One time, a knockout punch.

He stepped back, glanced at the other two in the room then looked down at her, crumpled on the floor. "I'm out," he said. "When she wakes up tell her I'm not interested. Tell her I'm not a snitch, I won't pay any attention if she goes through with this thing, but tell her if she comes after me it won't end well." He stood silent for a moment, expecting a comment or a question, anything. Nothing was said and he left.

Miller had retired at fifty-eight. Why hadn't he stayed retired? That's what he thought about as he drove home, a twelve-hour drive.

The invitation arrived like this: a guy who knew a guy who knew a guy knocked on his door one afternoon and said Deena Hoke wanted him for a job she had lined up. Miller should have played stupid or claimed he was somebody else or just slammed the door. But he hadn't. He'd been living in a small town on the Missouri-Iowa border for just over two years, in a small, forgotten farmhouse on a forgotten corner of an immense corporate farm where he paid rent once a year—cash—to a guy who collected rent once a year. That guy never offered a receipt and Miller never asked for one.

He didn't ask the guy who knew a guy who knew a guy how he'd found him. He should have.

Dutch Miller associated with no one, nobody bothered him, he kept his nose clean and paid cash for what few bills he had. He watched a lot of TV, did a little fishing, a little reading, took walks and worked on keeping the past in the past.

After the knock on his door—a rare thing—he'd listened to the guy who knew a guy who knew a guy, all the time knowing he knew better than to listen. Who was this guy? He never found out. He knew the name Deena Hoke, but that name came with baggage, most of it negative. He'd been bored living on the Missouri-Iowa border, and a little lonely, so he made a mistake. He thought about those things on the drive back home.

Dutch knew Deena's husband was dead. He'd heard the rumors that Deena had killed him and a friend of his. Those rumors were a couple years old.

When Deena's eyes fluttered open the room was empty. Her eye was swollen and her head throbbed. She knew the job was queered ... word would get out and there was no way she could get anyone interested again. To soothe her rage she went on a bender. Meth and coke were available, so she got some. Weed? Why not? Alcohol? Lots. Going on a week later she was sitting in a dive bar, late afternoon, drinking, talking too loud, and she mentioned Dutch Miller's name to the bartender, like he wanted to listen to her anymore than he already had. There was a guy in the back, sitting alone, reading a newspaper, half listening. Hearing Miller's name he folded his paper, chewed on his lip, got up and walked to the bar and offered to buy Deena Hoke a drink. It wasn't a tough sell.

She had one on him and mentioned she'd like another and that was okay with him. He motioned to the bartender for two more. When that one was gone he said "You know Dutch Miller?" Deena got all quiet when he asked that, like she'd been offended. He watched her rummy brain try to do something with that question, but figured after another drink or two she'd forget all about it, and he was right.

Before the night was over he'd seen her without any clothes on, told her that he was falling for her and they might make it as a couple, and she'd told him that she knew Dutch Miller and Miller had ruined her perfectly-good plan.

"Where'd you find Dutch Miller?" he asked her. She'd already explained her plan, which he listened to patiently. He told her it sounded "solid," but it wasn't. He waited for her to shut up, which she rarely did, but he was patient. After he showed her how much he was falling for her, she answered all his questions.

His name was Dwight Thomlinson and he knew a guy who had been looking for Dutch Miller for a long, long time. The next morning he called the guy and asked if he was still looking for Dutch Miller and when the guy said "yes," Dwight told him he had good news.

It took Dwight a day-and-a-half to find Deena's guy, the guy who knew a guy who knew a guy. When he found the guy—a fat old man who insisted on being called "Big Tim"—Dwight gave the guy two thousand dollars to tell him where he'd found Dutch Miller. Then he told the guy they should never see each other again. Ever. Then he ditched Deena. What did he need her for?

Dutch Miller's reputation was made when he killed two lunkheads in a wildlife preserve in Arkansas and drove off with their money and the drugs they'd stolen. The guy who owned those drugs was middle management—worked out of Cincinnati—but he had influence both up and down the ladder, and he was impressed when Miller looked him up and returned his money and the drugs. Dutch had been paid handsomely to end the two lives; he figured the smart thing to do was return the money and the drugs to their rightful owner, which he did. He liked things squared up. The middle manager offered Dutch Miller a job, Dutch declined, which disappointed the guy, but the middle manager was relieved to have his drugs back so he gave Dutch some money out of his own pocket and told him if he was ever in the neighborhood ...

That guy never told anyone, but he was afraid of Dutch Miller the first time he laid eyes on him.

Miller drifted around, a freelancer. He wasn't popular, he wasn't friendly, he associated with no one and anyone claiming they'd had a genuine conversation with him was lying. But he was eminently reliable. Nobody who worked with him was ever disappointed. He moved often, and before each move he'd find himself some kind of preacher, some kind of evangelist, and unburdened himself.

"Why am I like this?" he'd ask them. "Why do I live like this, doing these wrong things? What's the matter with me? Why don't I feel anything?" He'd dive right in, telling them everything, and when he talked like that, his confessor would usually get all serious, head down, ask him to pray and tell him God can forgive anything, but only if. The "only if" was always the deal killer. Miller would leave behind some significant cash with each person who'd listened to his story, then explain how revealing anything about him would be a terrible mistake for the confessor, his family, and his parish. Then Dutch would disappear.

Older, all that bouncing around began to bother him. It bothered him there was nothing in his past he wanted to remember, and it bothered him that his future looked like his past.

In his time at the Missouri-Iowa border he grew fascinated—captivated, actually—with two things: gangster movies and meditation.

He watched a lot of TV, and stumbled onto foreign gangster movies: Japanese, Korean, Chinese, Filipino ... Indian. He was mesmerized. These movies preached a kind of honor that appealed to him. The gangsters had a code. They were sworn to some version of family. They had rituals and ceremonies and adhered to them. He lacked those things in his life.

Meditation?

Out for a drive the spring after he arrived, with no particular destination, he drove into Fairfield, Iowa, home of The Maharishi University and the epicenter of Transcendental Meditation in the U.S. He got hooked. It was something real to aspire to; it was soothing. It made him feel noble. It required—and this fit perfectly into Miller's lifestyle—it required no one other than himself. Him. Alone. He bought books on meditation, attended lectures every time he returned, which was once or twice a year, and breathed deeper and grew calmer with his new awareness. His mind linked the gangsters in the movies and their rituals and their code of conduct with this meditation. It made perfect sense to him. He meditated ... or at least he'd learned to sit silently for an hour a day. Sometimes more.

Dwight Thomlinson called the guy he notified, told him he needed his help to get to Dutch Miller, and that guy was on the road an hour later.

Deena Hoke pieced it together slowly. After the second day Dwight didn't show up she got mad as hell. She laid off the drugs a bit and realized she'd been foolish. She thought real hard about the questions Dwight had asked her and tried to remember how she'd answered. The guy who knew a guy who knew a guy? She went to him, they drank a bit, she cried on his shoulder and when he finally fessed up that he'd told Dwight where he'd found Dutch Miller, Deena sobered up real fast, held a gun to his head and told him she understood that two thousand dollars is two thousand dollars, but she was disappointed in him. She told him that going forward he had to actually shut his trap. He promised he would.

Deena knew a guy—a big guy with no brains and nothing to do—and told him about some big money near the Missouri-Iowa border and how they could get it. She invited him to her place and took off all her clothes and asked him if he liked what he saw and he said he sure did. Then she told him about the guy who knew a guy who knew a guy and that he'd have to be taken care of eventually—he was okay with that—and then she said they had to get to the Missouri-Iowa border and get that money. She talked it up quite a bit. It was gonna be easy and rewarding.

Dutch Miller was sitting in a diner, eating breakfast, when a guy walked in and Dutch knew immediately that the guy was trouble. How did he know?

"I know trouble before trouble starts," he told a preacher in Indiana once. The preacher was very, very successful, a regular on another preacher's TV show, and had a great big church that filled up twice on Sundays. This preacher also had a taste for drink and drugs. "I could use you," the preacher had told Dutch. "You got a gift," the preacher said. "Your perceptions, that's a gift from God." This preacher, himself, needed someone confess to, and he'd confessed a bunch of stuff to Dutch, which made Dutch uncomfortable. The preacher offered Dutch a security position with his ministry. Dutch turned him down. He offered it several more times. Dutch said he'd think about it, then relocated.

The guy who walked into the diner was Dwight Thomlinson and he took a seat in a booth and twenty minutes later a truck pulled into the parking lot and a guy got out of that truck and walked into the diner, stopped at the cashier and asked for a cup of coffee, then walked over and sat opposite Dwight Thomlinson.

When he was seventeen, Randall Bell walked away from a juvenile facility in Florida where he was being detained until his eighteenth birthday. He'd been arrested twice, both times for home invasion. He kicked around for a couple months, made his way up to Virginia, and that's where he met Dutch Miller, a cocky drug dealer in his late twenties, who would do about anything for money.

Randall Bell was an anomaly. He appeared to be a hick, which in fact he was, but his IQ was off the charts; he excelled in all academics and made it look easy. It's not a nice thing to say, but his people were pure trash. As a small child, as a boy, he was an introvert; then he was an introverted adolescent. The summer between his sophomore and junior years he transformed into a troubled, introverted teenager. The incident that put him away was a spur-of-the-moment thing; he beat up an elderly couple pretty bad and the next morning was caught in their car. His family didn't show up in the courtroom, didn't visit him at the detention center, never called and never wrote. When he walked away from the juvenile facility, as far as he was concerned he had no family.

In Virginia he tried to steal junk food from a rural convenience store where Dutch Miller's team were selling drugs from behind the cash register. He was, of course, caught, and turned over to Dutch Miller, who slapped him around a little and then—seeing something in the boy—put him to work. Randall Bell doubled Miller's business in a year and they became something like father and son.

Two years later, Bell, who by then knew damn near everything about Dutch Miller's businesses, shot Miller in the back of the head and drove off in Miller's car with around $350,000 in cash. He left the car at a shopping mall in Youngstown, Ohio, keys in the ignition.

Two days later he stepped off a bus in Kansas City, Missouri, and from that point on he introduced himself as Dutch Miller. Why he chose that name is left to those with extensive psychological training.

The Dutch Miller name carried a bit of mystique. First there was the real Dutch Miller, the drug dealer who'd been shot and robbed. That story was common and for that reason didn't last long. But the second Dutch Miller? Randall Bell's Dutch Miller?

Among those clinging to the bottom rung of criminality's ladder, *that* Dutch Miller was the cowboy who could, would, and did.

That Dutch Miller was low-key, quiet, smart and dependable. He was around when good money was to be made and when the good money was made he disappeared with his share, sometimes with more. Word was he could speak Spanish and disappeared into Mexico. Word was he could blend in with anybody anywhere anytime. Word was he did not show fear and did not panic. Word was you couldn't spot him in a crowd totaling three. Word was he was polite, gracious, and deferential, never spent a dime he didn't have to, lived like a hermit and had a bundle of money.

Word was word was word was. His name didn't come up often, but when it did, folks listened.

Dwight Thomlinson had heard about the money. He'd been told about the money and even met folks that claimed ownership of some of that money. Those folks held some sway in Thomlinson's world and he knew they would appreciate—reward—the person who found it. That was Dwight's angle.

Deena Hoke? Deena was not right in the head. She had trouble controlling her temper. Paranoid? Probably. None too bright. The intoxicants she used too frequently didn't help. But she'd decided she wanted something out of Dutch Miller and would decide what it was after she had his scalp in her hands.

On the way to that small town on the Missouri-Iowa border, she talked non-stop about how, once there, she'd observe Miller for a day or two while she fine-tuned the plan. "We'll just kick back, have some drinks and roll around in bed," she told her new partner. He loved hearing that. She did all the driving. He had a couple-too-many DUI's and was due to show up in court a couple months ago. He drank, she drove.

Dwight located Dutch Miller in two days. Miller, aware that trouble had arrived, helped him by spending both days shopping along the tiny main street, something he almost never did. He stopped at the two strip malls and had lunch and dinner out. These things were unusual for him, and had he been asked why, he would have said "instinct," because that's what it was. He knew those guys were looking for him and thought it better they find him sooner rather than let the whole thing drag on. He watched them follow him home one evening, trailing behind a quarter mile or so, then drive right past his lane. He felt good about that.

On her first day on the Missouri-Iowa border, Deena Hoke saw Dwight Thomlinson walking down the main drag and knew right away she had to act fast. Her and the muscle had checked into a motel; she'd left him with a bottle and cable TV and told him she was going to look at the lay of the land. She parked her car and caught Thomlinson in front of a hardware store. He smiled and she didn't.

"What?" he said. "You think I cut you out?"

Deena Hoke wasn't drunk, but she'd been on maintenance amphetamines for a couple days. "I ought to shoot you where you stand," she said.

He frowned. "Come on, Deena," he said, then smiled and said "turn around."

Deena turned around and saw the guy Dwight Thomlinson was partnering with. He looked smarter than her guy. She turned back to Thomlinson and said "I want a share."

Thomlinson nodded. "Okay, that's not unreasonable, so let's talk."

Miller's farmhouse was about three miles outside of town, down a private lane. It had electricity paid for, unknowingly, by the corporation that owned the farm. Same with water, which was low pressure but good enough. The septic tank worked. In the winter Miller's truck was parked in a dilapidated barn the corporation thought had been torn down years earlier.

For two days he drove back and forth—home to town … town to home—until he was confident he'd revealed his whereabouts to Dwight Thomlinson. He put a case of beer in the bed of his pickup while Thomlinson watched from across the street, then went back into the store and bought another case. It was all show; Dutch Miller did not drink alcohol. Ever. He'd never been an idea man, but he'd seen movies where guys with real brains could sort through their difficulties. This had convinced him that he could do it, too, or at least learn to.

In American movies, tough guys drank all the time, smoked all the time, yakked away all the time. In the movies he'd been watching nobody did that. He figured that was smarter.

His Deena sighting was strictly luck. He was at one of the town's four stoplights when she walked right in front of his truck, never glancing left or right. She looked wired. Miller took that as a positive.

The first night after he'd seen both Thomlinson and Deena, Miller stayed up late, light on in the living room, watching a movie about a gangster hunted by rivals and receiving no help from his family. It looked like his family had sold him out. Then it turned out they were being threatened by the same rivals and were scared. Then they threw in with the rivals. Then they tried to help him, but he was afraid they were setting him up. Eventually the gangster who was being hunted just killed them all, family and foes. That's what Dutch would do.

The next day he stayed home, listening to cars pass on the road down the lane. He meditated in the morning and in the afternoon paged through a book on budo and serenity.

They came at night.

The banging on his door happened about ten. There was shouting. "Mister! Hey! Mister!" He waited, and the banging on the door increased "There's an accident out on the two-lane. We need help! We need your help now!"

When he opened the door, Dwight Thomlinson was pointing a gun at him; Miller didn't even look surprised and Dwight could see that. That was unnerving.

Miller backed into the room and Thomlinson stepped in and the guy who had met Thomlinson at the diner stayed by the door.

Miller sat down on his couch and nobody said a word. Eventually Miller pointed at a closet right next to the door, right where Dwight Thomlinson was standing, and Thomlinson opened that door and smiled. There were two large duffel bags in there, one stacked on the other.

"That's my money," Miller said.

Why did that make Thomlinson feel so funny?

"There's close to four hundred thousand in each of them bags," Miller said. "That's what you're here for, isn't it?"

Thomlinson looked all around the room, slowly, wondering where Miller's gun was. He kept his gun on Miller, kept his eyes on Miller, and talked over his shoulder to his partner.

"Look in them bags, will you, Errol?" he said.

Errol started to move, but hadn't put one foot into Miller's living room when two shots hit him, both from his right. He fell hard, into the living room. Thomlinson backed up a step, then two, then watched as Deena Hoke stepped into the room. She looked at Miller, looked at Dwight and nodded, then shot Errol two more times. For Deena, good-and-dead beat dead any day.

"Get the bags," Thomlinson said.

Deena glanced at the bags, walked right past them and dropped the barrel of her gun on Dutch Miller's forehead.

"Deena, that ain't part of this plan," Thomlinson said. "Stop," he said. "Deena, back up."

"I'm gonna kill Dutch Miller," she said.

Miller grabbed her wrist and swung her around, using her body as a shield, then grabbed the gun out of her hand, pointed and pulled the trigger, managing to shoot a startled Dwight Thomlinson two times in the chest. Miller turned her around again and punched Deena Hoke in the face, twice. Her eyes rolled back and she went limp.

He walked over to Thomlinson. He was shot good enough.

Miller tied up Deena's wrists real tight, then tied her ankles, left her on the floor and went outside. Two cars. He figured it was Dwight's in the yard. Deena's was most likely down the lane a bit.

He went back in, sat on her chest and slapped her until her eyes flickered.

"You alone?" he asked.

She gasped, struggled just a bit, looked up at him. "I'm alone," she said. "It's just me and Dwight."

He wrapped both hands around her neck, leaned down on her and squeezed until he thought he ought to stop.

"You really come alone?" he asked.

She answered every question he asked, then she followed orders, calling her guy, telling him to be ready, she'd be there in twenty minutes.

Twenty minutes later they pulled up at the hotel. Her muscle jumped in the car and when she was back out on the highway the muscle felt a barrel press against the back of his head.

"Do not turn around," Miller said. "Put your hands on top of your head and leave them there. If they come down for any reason I have to shoot you."

Back at Miller's house they strolled into the farmhouse, When the guy saw the body in Miller's living room he jumped, pushed at Deena's back, tried to go around, and Dutch Miller shot him three times, twice in motion, once as he lay on the floor. Then Miller handed the gun to Deena. She looked at it, pointed it at Miller's head and pulled the trigger once, twice, then once more. Nothing. When she looked at Dutch Miller he was frowning. "Christ, Deena, did you think I'd give you a loaded gun?"

Then he hit her once more, and down she went.

When Deena came to, Dutch Miller was standing in the doorway. Her wrists were bound. Her ankles were bound. She was on the floor and looked up at Dutch and started crying.

"I'm conflicted," Miller said to her. He waited for a reply but none came, she was crying too hard. He'd been thinking about how he'd killed her husband and the other guy years earlier. It had been a contract job. He figured she'd never known. He thought it was funny that he was probably going to have to kill her now. It was like in the movies, the family thing and how you can think it's over but it's not. There's always somebody else coming at you, because everyone has a role to play and they have to stay in that role because that's where their honor is. The honor is in accepting your role and being proud of the way you handle the responsibility of what you have to do.

He didn't think it was honorable for Deena Hoke to be crying.

"I'm going to have to kill you," he said, and she wailed.

Minutes later he walked out to her car, drove it up to the house so the front bumper kissed the front of the house, shut it off and got out. Then he went and got Dwight's car, drove it up on the pad that sat outside the front door and got the bumper to kiss the door frame. He got out, walked around and went in the back door, came out with a gas can and poured gasoline over both cars. He went back in, sat on the couch perfectly still, silent, eyes closed, breathing slowly, counting each inhale, each exhale. He counted close to five hundred, then grabbed the duffel bags and carried them out to his truck. Back into the house one more time, scattered all his clothes around the house, doused the place and then got in his truck and drove a hundred feet or so down the lane and waited there, foot on the brake, until he could see flames climbing the curtains in the front window. Then he drove off.

He'd lived there two years. There'd never been a photo on a wall, a calendar on a door, or a piece of mail delivered.

Miller drove to Cleveland, three or four miles-an-hour over the speed limit all the way. He got breakfast from a fast-food window in Springfield, Illinois, and dinner near Dayton, the same way. When he arrived in Cleveland, he became Randall Bell again. The idea for the switch came to him during the drive and to him—him coming up with that idea—that showed he was getting smarter. He credited it to watching those gangster movies and meditating. All that had made him more receptive to his own personal skills, his own personal truth. It was the circle of life, or something like that. He'd seen it in the gangster movies. He read about it in the books he bought in Fairfield, Iowa. At one of the lectures he'd attended in Fairfield he'd been told to become truly yourself, "you have to do the work."

He'd done the work, he was sure of it. That's why he became Randall Bell again.

In Cleveland Randall Bell paid cash for a laundromat—he bought it cheap and fixed it up. The guy he bought it from handed him off to an accountant who could make Randall Bell look like an upstanding businessman.

Within a year Randall Bell met a nice woman. He met her renting gangster movies in the shop she ran; it offered all kinds of Korean stuff: food, cosmetics, magazines, cheap dishes and cheap glasses and coffee cups; she was Korean. Her English wasn't too good, but that didn't bother him. She described her life to him in her pidgin English and he listened, trying to understand, realizing her life had been tough, like his own. She'd had to scramble to survive; she'd had to start over multiple times. When he told her about his life—leaving out the killing—she listened closely, nodding.

They married. The ceremony was small, held in a community center that catered to immigrants. It was him, her, her mother, an aunt who barely spoke, and an officiant, the whole thing in Korean. He liked it. It was a simple ceremony and some sort of noodle soup that was required at Korean weddings was served. He liked that too.

After the wedding her mother lived with them, which was fine with Bell. Finally, family again.

His wife and mother-in-law told him they had some family in Minnesota and they went there every year to hold some traditional ceremonies, or rituals, or something like that. His wife insisted they go. "Got to do," she said. She said that multiple times: "Got to do." Sounded like more ceremonies to him, and it sounded like it was centered on family. He figured some honor was involved too. It sounded good.

They went in the late fall, leaving on a Friday at noon, driving continually for twelve-plus hours until, on Minnesota State Route 1, an hour or two east of Fergus Falls, they got lost. The wife was driving.

Mother and daughter got talking in their other language, arguing maybe, then they started laughing with each other. Bell laughed too. Everybody was smiling and excited and they drove on until Bell's wife said she had to pee. The mother-in-law started laughing and his wife was trying not to laugh because she had to pee so bad. Bell said he could take a pee, too, so they pulled off on a small lane, a logging road, and his wife got out, ran to the side of the car, pulled down her jeans and squatted, laughing hard. He cracked his door and was starting to get out when he felt the hairs on his neck stand up.

He ducked. A gun went off, a bullet whizzing past his head and blasting through the windshield. He swatted with his right arm and his right hand, got a hand on the gun then dove over the seat and put his other hand to his mother-in-law's neck and squeezed. That stopped her screaming. He looked to his wife, standing up, scrambling, then he shot his mother-in-law in the head and jumped out of the car.

His wife was running down the rutted lane. It would have been much smarter, he thought, to run through the brush. Why didn't she think to run through the brush?

He got back to Brainerd, Minnesota, without incident, worrying about that windshield the whole time. A cop seeing that windshield would be trouble. In Brainerd he stole a car and drove to Chicago. He dumped the car and from there it was Amtrak to Cleveland.

The remains of his wife and mother-in-law would be found in the spring. By then he was living in Tampa, where he'd bought a carwash. He would sell that carwash for cash a year later, below asking price, and drift toward Pensacola. In Pensacola he called himself Brad. Sometimes Brad Miller, sometimes Brad Bell. That turned out to be a problem when he was T-boned at the corner of Main and Palafox by a drunk.

When he woke up in the hospital there was a man sitting on a chair, doing what looked like a crossword puzzle in the newspaper.

"Say there," the man said when he saw Bell awake. He pulled his chair closer, smiled, and introduced himself as Detective Ray Yustiz. "You," he said, "have a couple names—at least that's what we've been able to dig up so far—and we'd like to know why that is."

Brad Bell, that's what Miller thought. *Brad Bell. Go with Brad Bell.*

He felt tight in the chest, weak all over. One leg was elevated. His neck was wrapped up real tight. He struggled to crane his neck and see his body; when he did he saw his right arm was in a cast, wrist to shoulder. He tried to pull his left hand into sight; he heard jingling and his hand jerked to a stop about mattress level. He was cuffed to the bed.

He looked at Yustiz.

"You don't have a driver's license," Yustiz said. "And where in heaven's name did you get those license plates?" The detective's smiled faded. "You're not insured," he said, "and the title isn't in the truck or in your wallet and we haven't gone into that little bungalow you're living in to see if it's there because we're not going in without a legal search warrant." The smile was gone. "You could agree to allow us to go in, you know, and tell us where we could find that title."

The cop stood up and looked down at Brad Bell, shoved his hands into his pockets and shook his head slowly and took a deep breath.

Bell went into defense mode. No expression. Didn't say a word. Closed his eyes slowly and kept them closed.

"You know how long you been in here?"

Bell didn't answer. Didn't open his eyes.

"Two days," the cop said. "And there is so little we know about you, and so much we have to find out."

Bell fell asleep again. It didn't take much effort.

When he woke up again it was a day later. At least it felt like that to Brad Bell. He opened his eyes slowly, thinking he had to be careful. He heard some murmuring, shuffling feet, then somebody walked into the room.

Detective Ray Yustiz appeared over his bed, staring down at him, hands shoved into his pockets, lips tight. "Morning," he said.

No reply.

"You're an interesting guy," Yustiz said. He turned around, said something in Spanish to somebody near the door, then turned back, looked down and said, "The name Dutch Miller mean anything to you?"

THE ASSASSIN'S PORTRAIT

Nina Wachsman

"**Y**ou are most meticulous with the tools of your trade," the old man said, as I packed away brushes and paints into their worn wooden box.

"I have to be, my success depends upon it," I said, wiping my paint-stained fingers with a ragged cloth. "Besides, it would not do to have any evidence left at the scene of the crime, now, would it?"

I disliked the old codger, even though he did have good cause to order both the portrait and the death of his son-in-law. I took a last look at the insouciant smirk of the man in the portrait. Only in oils would his charming smile be seen, since by now it had faded into the grimace of death when I had completed his portrait. I wondered whether his long-suffering wife would reminisce over it fondly, recalling earlier days, before her husband revealed his true nature.

The old man stood alongside me and joined me to gaze at the portrait. "It is astonishing how life-like you have made him, though we both know he was never as noble as you have painted him."

He sighed and placed a folded document into my hands. "Here is the deed conveying ownership of my estate to your uncle. He drives a hard bargain, the blackguard, but my daughter's happiness is worth it."

He did not take his eyes off the glistening portrait, its veneer still wet, as he added, "I am tempted to burn it, so she can forget him, but I will not. It will be a legacy to my grandson, and should put to rest any remaining rumors about his father."

I placed the valuable document into a small leather pouch inside a special pocket concealed in my skirts. My uncle had extorted this nobleman's estate as the price of the assassination, and I shrugged off any guilt for my part in it. The cad would have probably lost his wife's estate at the gaming tables, anyway. However, I did think Uncle was growing a bit too bold in pricing my services. It was never wise to cause clients to grumble; it would not do to draw any attention to our enterprise.

A servant entered silently and showed me out. My traveling bag stood by the door, and I allowed the footman to carry it to the waiting coach, while I kept hold of my paint box.

He grows too big for his breeches. His portrait should be magnificent.

A slip of paper, with a phrase and a name, conveyed the subject of my new commission, along with instructions and an address where and when I should appear.

Light streamed into the morning room, and I took another sip of tea as I held the paper up close. The name was one I recognized, as would anyone in this year of 1858: a Whig MP for Bristol, known as the Reformer. I imagined he had earned great enemies among the powerful, and it was certain he had little suspicion of the true intent of those colleagues who had commissioned his portrait as a gift. I rose and tossed both the envelope and its contents into the fire, ringing for my servants to prepare my things for a journey.

Luckily, Bristol was now connected to London by the Great Railway, so I was to be spared a long journey jostling over the moors with my paintbox in my lap. I placed the new hat gently over my dark brown hair, careful not to disturb the artfully arranged curls that had pained my maid to create. The large carpet bag and trunk had been packed and were ready for transport, and I had ordered a smart new ensemble for the journey.

I had learned that men of power judged women solely by their appearance, and so I had been just as meticulous about mine as I was about the contents of my paintbox. I drew on a new pair of grey leather gloves, a perfect match for my traveling suit, and took a last look at myself in the large hallway mirror. With the objectivity I used for studying my subjects, I deemed I still had several years of good looks and a softness that would disarm most men of Society. My eyes, a cold blue, were the only hint of the steel inside me, deadened to sympathy for those I been ordered to paint.

I entered a first-class compartment and made myself comfortable, carefully positioning my cherished paintbox on the seat beside me. I did not want or expect company and the snippets of countryside flashing by the window were hypnotic, relaxing me into a state of internal contemplation.

The rocking of the carriage was as soothing as a cradle, although I have no memories of ever being soothed or caressed by a mother. She had died in bearing me, devastating my stern and exacting father, who therefore bore me no love. Nevertheless, my father did not shirk his duty towards me, and I was attended by efficient servants and tutors to ensure I was suitably trained as a lady of my station should be.

Drawing and painting had interested me from an early age, and my tutors dutifully reported my talent to my father. When they recommended the hiring of a drawing master, his brother intervened. My uncle had gained some notice in his youth for his painting, and offered to become my drawing master and painting tutor, which enabled him to move into our house. My uncle, Sir F__________ was in need of a patron and a home, since he had already spent both his dead wife's fortune and his own, on gambling and other dubious activities. My father, who had secluded himself from society after the death of my mother, had no knowledge of the shadiness of his brother's reputation, and allowed him to take residence and become my mentor.

It was Uncle who first noticed how flowers faded as I painted them, losing all of their petals and dying just as the painting was completed. Knowing full well I would be the only heir to my father's estate, my uncle wanted to test my powers, and convinced my father to let me paint his portrait. Still hanging over the mantlepiece in the drawing room, it depicted a man full of power and strength, so unlike the shadow he became as I sucked the life from him into my work.

Talent and skill, fueled by some strange power, enabled the brush in my hand to drain the vitality out of my subjects, like a legendary succubus. I put a proprietary hand on my paint box, stroking the smooth wood as if it were a cherished pet. It was miraculous, as face and form became more animated when I daubed paint from palette to brush to canvas. At each sitting, the color lessened in my subject's cheeks while it seemed to infuse into the painted surface before me. As a man's eyes dulled at each sitting, his image beneath my brush, sparkled to life, full of secrets and desires.

Uncle was there to guide me. My gloved hand clenched at the thought of his thin-lipped smile, and his hooded, depraved eyes. As the executor of my father's estate, he controlled my income, and through his shady connections, arranged my commissions. Appreciation of my work as a portraitist was growing as rapidly as the secret demand for my services as an assassin. A commission for my portraits had become highly exclusive, and awfully expensive. I should be satisfied with Uncle's management, since I lived independently, and he never challenged my expenditures, but I loathed him.

When I arrived in Bristol, I was pleased with the house where the sittings would be; the room set up for me was large and sunny, with windows overlooking the garden. However, my discomfort arose with my subject at the very first sitting.

He did not enter a room like a gentleman, he stormed into it like a soldier, declaring, "I have no time for such nonsense."

"Your cravat is loose, and your hair is untidy. It does not suit the image of a statesman," I said calmly. My paintbox was open, and as I studied his face, I observed his skin tones, mentally checking off the need for yellow ocher, alizarin crimson, and raw sienna. Perhaps some cadmium blue for the shadow of the beard at the jawline.

Self-conscious, his hand went to his neck to confirm my observation. His heavy dark eyebrows (raw umber, Prussian blue) descended over dark brown eyes, as he glowered at me. "What is the image of the statesman then? Serene and blasé perhaps?"

I shook my head. "Trustworthy and kind, I should think."

We were interrupted by a whirlwind which sent papers flying, toppled a vase and revealed to have been caused by a little tow-headed girl. The politician's brows relaxed into a straight line, and his lips curved into a smile. "My dear, why do you disturb us?"

The little girl grabbed her father's leg, and half hiding herself behind him, peeked at me. "I wanted to see the lady who would be painting you. Nanny thought she was odd, and I wanted to see for myself."

Despite myself, I smiled. I was indeed very odd, but not by outward appearance. The Reformer pointed to me. "She does not look unusual, does she? She is distinguished by her skill, which unfortunately, many like Nanny, might consider odd in a woman, but you should not. I should hope someday you should discover some talent or interest that will distinguish you."

"Could I be in the painting with you, do you think?" the little girl asked. Her father had relaxed his tense pose, the fabric of his coat less taut across his shoulders, as he looked at me. "We will have to ask the artist if it can be arranged. In the meantime, find something to draw and practice and perhaps *you* can paint me after her work is finished."

The blonde curls danced on the little girl's head as she clapped her hands, and without a curtsey or a goodbye, ran from the room. "As you can see, I allow my daughter a great many liberties. I advocate such freedom for all women to explore their talents and cultivate their intellect. I do indulge my daughter more than is customary, I suppose, but I justify it because she has been left without the loving care of a mother. I lost my wife when she gave birth to her."

My subject's words and the interruption of his motherless child made my hands tremble. Mechanically, I said, "I am sorry for your loss." Then, after considering what he had said, I added, "Your views are quite different from most powerful men."

He looked pleased at my observation. "Have you painted many powerful men?"

"Many who thought they were powerful," I said, although I realized, too late, that my answer was bound to stimulate his curiosity. Still disconcerted by his child's appearance and his request to having her included in the painting, I decided to continue talking of the past. "My subjects, including my own father, have been notable men, who have either stridden or sauntered into their first sitting, intending to convey their superiority to inferiors like me. Whether they had lived up to their own opinions of themselves is not for me to say."

I had relished how humbled they had become by their last sitting, when the shadow of death loomed. Although ignorant of my power, they were beholden to me until I completed their portrait—to me, a woman who faced them with only a paintbrush, and yet had the power to deplete them.

As our conversation ebbed, the Reformer settled into a pose which seemed natural to him, with his head cocked to one side, one hand at his waist, standing with his weight upon the one hip. I dipped my brush into raw sienna thinned with linseed oil and sketched in the pose. I liked the way the light hit upon his face, outlining the length of his Roman nose and the chiseled cliffs of his cheekbones. I had not had the time to arrange a backdrop, but the trees and rolling hills faintly appearing through the panes of the window behind him presented a fitting background. I would paint thunder clouds instead of blue skies; it suited him better.

"The sameness to your subjects must challenge your creativity." His hand strayed from his hip to his waistcoat. I could see him fingering the pocket watch and resisting the urge to check the time.

I bit my lip. No one had ever commented in such a way to me. I was used to hearing either complaints or lewd suggestions from my subjects. I looked down at my palette as I answered him. "Do not concern yourself over me. I paint what I am paid to."

My subject raised one eyebrow. "You do not subscribe to the new thinking? To paint for yourself, to seek inspiration, rather answer the demands of a patron?"

"Do you suspect me of being a pre-Raphaelite?" I countered, careful not to reveal any opinion or hint of my thinking or personality.

"I should not fault you if you were. The appreciation of nature's beauty must be sustained, even during these times, with the advances of industry."

"Spoken like a statesman."

My comment made him chuckle, and our dialogue seemed to please him. He smiled at me. "I am quite enjoying this sitting. I did not expect it to be so."

Neither did I. I dallied around, erasing my sketches, so that little of the man's essence would flow into my canvas.

At the next sitting, when the little girl stormed once again into the room, my subject turned to me, his eyes soft and pleading. "Could you not find room for my little girl in this portrait? Besides being my inspiration, she is my reason for living. I am willing to compensate you fully for the extra work."

I pressed harder on the brush I was swirling into a thick gob of Prussian blue paint. I felt as if a hand was clutching my chest. "It will not please your colleagues, who commissioned this portrait."

"The devil with them! This is my portrait, not theirs. They seek to control my voice and now to control my image?" his brow was stormy as he strode away from the window and his position in the portrait.

I thought to buy some time by suggesting, "Perhaps I can communicate with my uncle, who had received the commission, and see what can be arranged."

"Agreed," he said, but to my relief, he did not regain his position. "We shall postpone further sittings until then."

"Until then," I repeated softly, and packed away my brushes carefully.

If I had hoped for a reprieve from the portrait by the suggestion that the subject's daughter should be added, I was to be disappointed. After reading the missive from Uncle, I nearly dropped in an uncharacteristic swoon to the floor.

Paint the girl instead. Her death will destroy him just the same, and there will be less suspicion cast over the portrait.

I was about to tear it up, and toss the fragments into the fireplace, when I read his added note, at the very bottom of the paper:

Do not think to refuse this commission, or you will pay dearly.

I clenched my teeth as I tossed the horrid letter into the fire. I would not harm a child, and I was determined that our association would end. If Uncle was prepared to take desperate measures, so was I.

I could not delay any longer; my host was aware I had received a response from my uncle. I had to resume the portrait of my subject, and I would claim the commission would not allow the inclusion of family.

For the past few days, I had the opportunity to learn more of the man I now referred to as the Reformer. When we dined together in the evenings, he shared his philosophies and the goals he hoped to accomplish as an MP, and I found myself in agreement with most of his opinions. Industry created opportunity, he argued, a universal truth applicable to every man *and woman* at any walk of life. He did not subscribe to the belief that a woman's mental capacity was inferior to a man's. In fact, according to his hypothesis, women had the natural ability to be more devious. He never suspected I was proof of his theory.

The Reformer argued and ranted on many topics during our discussions and as a result, I found I had more interest in subjects other than art. However, my lack of attention did not affect the strange power of my brushstrokes, and by the third sitting, my subject's nose seemed pointier and his cheekbones sharper.

"Do you not aspire to a higher level?" he asked me, licking his lips, which were pale and abnormally dry. "Portraiture is not the pinnacle of artistic expression. After all, you are not free to explore, when your parameters are limited to the subject of a portrait."

His words made me pause as I lifted my brush from the canvas. The painted image was defined enough to radiate the man's ferocity and sense of purpose. In comparison, the man who posed for me in the flesh looked like he needed rest. As his image grew more vivid in his portrait, in real life, he was becoming a shadow, and if I did not stop, it would not be long before he and the painting were finished.

"We are done for today," I announced, dousing my paintbrush into a jar full of turpentine.

"May I see?" he came towards the easel, which I swiveled towards him.

"My stars, you are incredible! I take back my previous assumption about your achievements. Do you really see me like that?" He wiped his hand across his brow. He was not as carefully shaven as he had been before, and he spoke with a slight rasp. "I confess, I no longer feel in possession of such power."

"Are you ill?" I asked, keeping my eyes on the brushes as I wiped them clean. I could not bear to see how much the fire had faded in his eyes.

"Just tired," he answered, "but I must preserve my strength if I am to live up to the image you have created of me."

"Then it is good we are done for the day. You will have more time to rest and recover."

In truth, I wondered if such would be the case. If I delayed in finishing the portrait, could his body recover its strength? Perhaps I could feign an illness to put off completing it, and postpone our sittings for a while?

I gazed at the painting on my easel. The Reformer was not like the others I had painted; he was a man of kindness and conviction, who could do great things for men and women if he were allowed to live. Evil men must have commissioned this portrait. The Reformer had stirred up one emotion in me I had thought I would never have. Empathy.

I could not condemn a man who was dedicated to the betterment of others, and who was responsible for the upbringing of a motherless daughter.

I gazed at my brushes and palette with horror. I wielded them as surely as the garrot and the blade and they were just as deadly. I had taken them up without qualm and now, belatedly, I was stricken with conscience. Uncle had already demonstrated he would not tolerate my change of heart. If he learned of my refusal to paint the little girl, he should be assuaged, for the time being, to see I had continued to paint the subject of my contracted submission.

I donned a cloak and hat and resolved to go for a walk to clear my head and devise an escape from my troubles. A footman rose to accompany me as I made for the door, but I waved him off, determined to enjoy the brisk damp air on my own.

As I followed the path into a small park, a cool wind came up, blowing my hair from my face and my cloak from my body. It was refreshing, as if a god-like breath had cleared away the cobwebs wrapped around my head, letting my thoughts roam freely.

I would not allow the Reformer to waste away. His conversation had stirred me; he had engaged my intellectual curiosity with new ideas of government, philosophy, and art. He had promised to take me to galleries where I might view the New Art, which he assured me, would lead to an artistic epiphany. Art should not seek to mirror the subject or to capture the soul, he claimed, but, like capturing fireflies in a jar, preserve only a fleeting moment.

Always diligent in the execution of my contracts, now the wind had changed, and I felt differently. I no longer wanted to be an assassin, only an artist. It was Uncle who kept me tethered to a steady stream of assassinations. He arranged the commissions under an assumed name, with which I signed the portraits, and carefully guarded our true identities as protection from possible prosecution. It was he who threatened me, and who was the threat to my future.

I walked with long hard steps, digging the heels of my boots deeper into the hard-packed dirt. Suddenly I stopped and smiled. I would ask my subject to postpone our next few sittings, so he could recover his strength and I could explore some new artistic directions.

It was time for me to paint a new portrait, this time of Uncle, the man who would never let me give up my role as an assassin.

It had begun to rain, and the wind blew sprinkles into my face. I squinted into the grey nothingness of the murky sky, conjuring the image of Uncle, etching each contour of his lean-boned face deeply into my mind. I stretched my fingers; they were aching to paint, and having extra canvas meant I could start his portrait immediately.

I swiveled round, regardless of the gusting of rain, eager to reach my rooms to begin painting. Although I would be working from memory, I was confident I had the power to bring the image of my uncle to life on the canvas.

Barely acknowledging my host's offer of warm food and drink, I shook off the wetness as best as I could and hung my sodden cloak on a peg. I informed him of my new plans, and begged his patience while I isolated myself in my rooms with canvas and paint. Mounting the stairs with unladylike speed, I unlocked my room and headed directly to my treasured paint box.

I would get a good start if I painted through the night, and I could break for a few hours to rest, then resume Uncle's portrait. A surge of energy coursed through me, gathering strength at my fingers where they connected with the brush and palette. I daubed and stroked pigment with great purpose and passion, until the face and form of my uncle was recognizable on the canvas. As each night passed, he became more defined.

During the day I worked on Uncle's portrait, but I managed to swirl enough paint on the Reformer's portrait, to render his face and figure less distinct. When the Reformer surprised me one day and caught sight of the change to his portrait, his eyes grew merry, and his face reflected good humor. "I suggest you leave my portrait as it is. It is more like the new art, where daubs and dots suggest face and form, instead of attempting to mirror life, and is infinitely more interesting. I wonder what my colleagues will think of it!" Along with his spirits, his voice had grown stronger, and he looked as if he was recovering his health.

I kept his attention on his portrait to avoid him looking at the other canvas that rested in the shadows, which, by chance, I had just removed from the easel before he entered the room. "I take it they do not appreciate the Impressionist approach. I should not be surprised they do not understand the interest in the large matter and the general character of a subject, instead of the defining details," I smiled and tilted my head towards him. "I have itched to explore their approach with a subject who is willing to experiment, and perhaps now I can."

Secretly, I hoped by moving away from a realistic depiction of the Reformer, I might spare him. By contrast, I had been painting Uncle as realistically as possible, and working constantly, even through the night, his portrait was now complete.

I pretended to be surprised when a servant interrupted us with a note for me.

"What news?" asked the Reformer, concern causing his bushy brows to furrow.

"My uncle has died, so his solicitor has notified me."

A hand meant to be comforting was placed on my shoulder. It was good he could not feel how I trembled with jubilation at the news. He said, "I had resented this portrait, but now I am happy I had consented to it, and I am glad to have made your acquaintance."

"I, too, am thankful you had agreed," I said, "you cannot contemplate how much this commission has affected me, or my work."

He stood up straighter at those words.

As I packed away my paints I added, "You should know, sir, the power of your influence upon me. I shall abandon my previous approach and never paint such portraits again."

RAT KILLER

Mark Mellon

Eliano was eleven when the stranger came to Matalo, a complete rarity in that tiny pueblo. Guzman had him sweep the porch while he washed glasses and mopped down the bar. He awkwardly swung the broom, taller than himself. Trotting hooves distracted him.

A man rode down the single dirt road, past the two dozen or so adobe huts and brush jacals that made up the Coahuilan hamlet. Mestizo dark, he dressed like a gringo in a sweat stained Stetson and denim brush jacket and pants. He rode a big stallion, a white and brown paint with a blond-black mane. Horse and man were dusty from long riding.

He halted before the tavern. "Hello, *chico*. Will you unsaddle my horse and brush him down for fifty centavos?"

Eliano grinned. "Certainly, *Señor*. Right away."

"Hold on. He works for me. You can't just take him away from his chores."

Guzman stood on the porch, walrus mustached, hands on hips, dirty white apron to his knees. The man dismounted.

"That's no way to talk to a customer."

"I'm not open until noon."

"You're open when I say you are."

Big, broad shouldered, his eyes were like black obsidian chips, a Colt '73 Peacemaker on his left hip, a bowie knife on his right. Guzman visibly withered under his glare. He bowed and gestured to the batwing doors.

"I'm always open to a gentleman."

The stranger handed the reins to Eliano along with fifty centavos.

"Feed him too."

Clutching the coins in his free hand, Eliano led the horse to the stables in back. The man stepped onto the porch.

"I smell coffee. Any chance of eggs with it?"

Guzman smiled and nodded. "Of course, *Señor*. I cater to hungry travelers. Step into my establishment."

The tavern was a long, low ceilinged, narrow room, furnished with a half dozen deal tables and handmade chairs. Boards set on empty whiskey barrels served as a bar. Stone jugs of mezcal, tequila, and rotgut whiskey were set on shelves behind the bar. Coffee boiled in a pot atop the wood stove in the kitchen.

The man sat at a table in a corner, facing the door. He took off his hat and put a silver five-peso piece on the table.

"I want bacon and tortillas too. I had a long ride from Piedras Negras."

Guzman scooped up the coin and eagerly nodded. "Yes, *Señor*. I have a nice, fresh fletch and corn tortillas made by the woman next door."

He served coffee in a clay mug that the man sweetened with molasses. Done with the horse, Eliano fetched his food. He ate quickly, but carefully, mopping his mustache clean with his kerchief edges.

"You must know the ranchers here. Do any have cattle for sale?"

Guzman smiled broadly, reassured now he knew the man's business. "I know every rancher for a hundred kilometers around Matalo. What kind of stock are you looking for?"

He sipped coffee. "I work for a Yankee syndicate with land in North Texas. They want local animals to breed with their Herefords so their offspring can endure life on the plains. I need strong stock, close to longhorns."

Guzman nodded sagely. "You want the Ortega brothers. They run at least ten thousand head at their ranch, all half wild."

The stranger pushed aside his tin plate. "Where's their ranch? I'll ride there."

"No need, *Señor*. They come every Saturday for my roast cabrito. All three brothers should arrive soon. I'll introduce you."

"You'll get a commission if things go well. A hundred pesos."

Guzman's small eyes widened at the prospect of such a large, completely unexpected profit.

"I see you're an experienced businessman, *Señor*. Would you like more eggs and bacon? Perhaps a complimentary shot of my best whiskey?"

"I'm full and it's too early to drink, but you should make more coffee. I like it."

"Immediately, *Señor*."

Guzman hurried to the kitchen. He took Eliano by an elbow and whispered. "You know where the Ortega ranch is, right?"

"Sure. Out past the Cerro Gordo, down a draw."

"Quiet, boy! Ride the mule there. Tell the brothers a Norteño's here, looking to buy cattle. Tell them he's got money. There's a peso in it for you."

"*Si, Patron.*"

Eliano went to the stables and slipped a bridle onto Guzman's small, ill-tempered mule. He pushed his straw sombrero down tight, hopped onto the mule's bare back, reins in his left hand, and urged the mule on with a switch.

He trotted into scrubby, semi-arid countryside, the horizon so wide it seemed infinite, a boy alone on a mule in an endless, empty landscape of rugged, low, yellow brown hills sparsely covered by spiny dagger plants, barrel cactus, and bristle topped yucca trees. Powerful heat pressed down like an inescapable hot iron.

Accustomed to the land, a native, Eliano rode without fear, eyes out for rattlesnakes. The surefooted mule covered ground, urged on by his switch. He passed the Cerro Gordo, an enormous gulley where a stream trickled at the bottom, a magnet for animals and hunters. Eliano rode down the draw that led to the Ortegas' ranch.

The Ortegas had a two-story house built from wood carted by teamsters all the way from Laredo where they lived with their multiple women and children. Eliano found them at a corral, drinking tequila even though it was still early.

"Ride him, Teo. Don't let a horse get the better of you."

Lazaro and Ysidro, the older brothers, sat on the corral's top fence posts. They urged on Teofilo, the youngest. He rode an unbroken stallion who wildly plunged and reared as he tried to throw his hated rider. Ysidro pulled his Smith & Wesson .38 from a black leather shoulder holster and fired a round into the air to stir the horse up more.

Lazaro, the oldest and steadiest Ortega, turned and saw Eliano. He grinned and pointed at the boy.

"Look. It's Eliano, the little bastard. What are you doing here? We didn't order whiskey or tequila."

Eliano whipped off his sombrero. "Guzman sent me, Don Lazaro. A Norteño's here. He has money and wants to buy cattle for rich Yankees. Guzman says you should come see him."

Lazaro nudged Ysidro. "A chance to make money on a Saturday."

Ysidro smirked. "Any time is fine with me."

"Hey, Teo," he shouted, "quit farting around on that old nag. We're going to relieve some Norteño asshole of his money."

Teofilo leaped backwards off the horse and landed nimbly on his feet. He shrugged his shoulders.

"*Porque no*, why not? I love taking gringos' cattle and their money. What could be sweeter than to sell them back their own stolen cattle?"

The brothers loudly laughed. Lazaro threw a peso to Eliano that the boy deftly caught and tucked inside his sombrero.

"We'll clean up first. Tell that fat bastard we'll be there in two hours. Now ride, *chico*."

Eliano turned the mule and lashed him back toward Matalo. The day grew hotter as he sped through the hills, fearful of the Ortegas' notoriously bad tempers.

When he reached Matalo, he rushed into the tavern, eager to share his important news. The man was eating a roast chicken Guzman had cooked without asking, desperate to curry favor with the taciturn man.

"The Ortegas said they'll be here in two hours, *Patron*."

Guzman cuffed him. "By all the saints, boy, can't you be discreet?"

"Don't hit him for doing what you told him to do."

Guzman flashed a conciliatory smile. "Of course, *Señor*. Just as you say. The boy's just impetuous."

"Most boys are. Come here, *chico*. Finish this chicken. Guzman, start cooking that cabrito you bragged about. That's why they're coming, remember?"

Guzman roasted goat meat over a charcoal bed outside in the back. Matalo was filled with roasting meat's smell, so delicious some wept, knowing they'd never enjoy such bounty.

The Ortegas announced themselves with loud whoops and pistol shots as they galloped into Matalo. They'd washed in a tin sitz bath, sprayed on cologne, and donned their charro outfits, broad sombreros, tight-fitting, short jackets, and flared pants, covered with intricate embroidery. Their saddles were studded with turquoise conchos; the bits had silver fittings.

They tethered their horses at a hitching post and stomped on high heeled boots into the tavern, big, well fed, young men. Lazaro's face lit up with exaggerated delight at the sight of the man. He held out his arms in welcome.

"So here's the fellow we came to see. *Bien encontrado, hombre!*"

The stranger rose and gravely shook hands with the brothers. He pointed to the table.

"Let's have a drink so we can introduce ourselves properly."

"Good idea," Ysidro said. "It's been an hour since I had one."

They sat down. Eager to see a successful deal concluded, Guzman fetched a jug of tequila and four clay mugs without asking. The man uncorked the jug and filled the mugs. Teofilo raised his in a toast, a smile on his handsome face.

"Thank you, *Señor*. I am Teofilo Ortega y Barros. These are my brothers, Ysidro and Lazaro."

"And who might you be, *Señor*?" Ysidro demanded.

"I'm Monte Page. I'm a cattle buyer for the XIT Ranch."

Ysidro slurped tequila. "What sort of puzzle are you? You speak Spanish like a Mexican and you're dark as one too, but you dress like a gringo and you have a gringo name."

Lazaro punched Ysidro hard on the shoulder, a blow the younger brother meekly suffered. "Ysidro, how many times have I told you to stop being so goddamned rude? Don't insult the gentleman before we even do business with him!"

Page smiled faintly. "I don't mind answering. I'm a Seminole. I live in the Big Bend now, but I grew up in Nacimiento here in Mexico. The XIT hired me because I know the country on both sides of the river."

"Ah, I've met some of your people before," Lazaro said. "Fine trackers, hunters, *vaqueros*. What can we do for you, *Señor* Page?"

"I want to buy a herd, a thousand head with at least a hundred ungelded bulls, the rawest, meanest, wild cattle you have, longhorns basically. The XIT plans to interbreed them with Herefords to get cattle tough enough to endure the North Texas winters."

"Gringos and their fancy ideas. They make me sick," Ysidro said.

"Quiet," Lazaro snapped. "We've got what you need, our own stock, tough enough to grub out a living in these godforsaken hills. We could round up a herd in about a week. The question is, what will you pay?"

"That's a lot of work, *Señor* Page," Teofilo said.

"These are my terms. Ten American dollars for each cow and twenty-five apiece for the bulls since they're what the XIT really wants. A total of eleven thousand, five hundred dollars, but I'll expect you to drive the herd to Eagle Pass so they can be shipped north by rail from there."

"Drive a bunch of wild cattle over two hundred kilometers for that amount? You're cheating us!"

"Shut up, Ysidro," Lazaro said. "The drive would take about a week more. We'd have to hire extra hands too. So why don't we agree on a round thirteen thousand American?"

"Extra hands don't cost that much. Twelve thousand, no more."

"Make it twelve thousand, five hundred and we'll give you our best stud bull," Teofilo said.

"Done."

Satisfied a proper deal had been struck after the requisite amount of haggling, Lazaro filled everyone's mug. "Let's drink to a new business partnership."

They raised mugs and drank. Page sipped tequila, as he had throughout. Guzman and Eliano brought out steaming plates heaped high with cabrito, pinto beans, and tortillas. Delighted by the fortune that just fell into their laps, the Ortegas feasted. They stuffed themselves with food and drank until they were sodden, lolling in their seats, stomachs about to pop from their frilled shirts. Page carefully watched, black eyes opaque.

"Tell me, Lazaro. Do you raise your own stock or buy outside to improve the breed?"

Ysidro sneered. "Why would we go to strangers to buy cattle? Nobody knows better than us Ortegas how to raise cattle. We can support a herd on land other people couldn't keep goats on."

Teofilo nodded. "*Es verdad*; it's true. We raised these cattle on our own. We've got the biggest herd in Northern Coahuila."

"All wearing your brand I suppose?"

The Ortegas stared at Page in drunken befuddlement.

"Yes, of course," Lazaro finally said. "Why do you ask, *Señor* Page?"

Page reached into a saddlebag by his chair. He pulled out an oval piece of cowhide, freshly cut from a carcass, and placed it on the table. A brand was plain upon the hide, a capital "B" with curved wings.

"Is this a joke, Page?" Ysidro shouted. "I don't think you're funny."

"That's the Flying B's brand, owned by Mr. Burrell in the Rosillos Mountains. I'm his rat killer, the one he sends to handle people like you. I cut that brand from a cow in your herd last night."

Lazaro's eyes went wide. "You son of a bitch. You killed one of our cows?"

"I cut her throat last night in a draw. You're sloppy thieves. You didn't even bother to alter the brand. I guess you thought they'd blend in with all the other cattle you stole across the river."

Despite their drunkenness, the Ortegas realized at last the hard-bitten Seminole had led them into a trap. They rose from their chairs and grabbed for their pistols. Ysidro snatched his Smith & Wesson from the shoulder holster and wildly snapped off a shot.

Yet Page was already on his feet, Peacemaker in hand. Calm and unruffled as before, he fired in rapid succession. The first shot caught Lazaro in the chest. His pistol dropped from his hand as he hit the floor.

Teofilo fired, but was too drunk to shoot straight. The bullet only creased the crown of Page's hat. Page shot Teofilo in turn. Ysidro ran for the door, but Page hit him twice before he reached it.

The Ortegas lay on the sawdust strewn floor, stained crimson by their pooling blood. Page reloaded and checked them. Ysidro and Lazaro were already dead. Only Teofilo still breathed. Too proud, too Mexican to beg for his life, he glared defiance.

"*Pinche gringo.* Your mother—"

Page shot him in the head. There was a terrible silence when the last gunshot's echoes faded away. The tavern was choked with burnt gunpowder's stench mingled with blood's salty tang. Guzman stood paralyzed, hands held apprehensively before his chest, certain he was about to die. Page holstered his pistol. From a leather poke, he carefully counted out five-peso coins and stacked them on a table.

"There's your fee. Tell the other ranchers not to come north of the river to steal cattle from the Flying B. That goes for the Ortegas too, if any of their sons grow older and get ideas about revenge. *Comprende*, understand?"

Guzman frenziedly nodded.

"Good. *Chico*, saddle my horse and bring him out front."

"*Si, Señor* Page."

Eliano ran to the stables. Page went behind the bar and picked up the Greener shotgun propped behind a barrel. He broke the shotgun open and removed the red paper cartridges.

"Just so you don't get ideas. Come outside, Guzman."

They went onto the porch. The dead men lay behind them, sprawled in ungainly poses on the floor. The dirt street was empty, everyone having fled inside their homes at the sounds of gunfire. They huddled on dirt floors, clutching handmade rosaries as they prayed to God, the Virgin Mary, and all the saints in heaven to spare them from being murdered. Eliano led the horse up to the porch, brushed, fed, and rested.

Page handed Eliano a five-peso coin. "Don't let Guzman take that from you. *Adios, chico.*"

He mounted his horse, urged the animal into a swift trot, and was gone. Guzman watched him leave. He spat into the dust.

"I'm sorry I ever saw you, you black Seminole son of a bitch. A measly hundred pesos to compensate me for the bloody mess you made and all the abuse I'll catch from the Ortegas. God damn you to hell, *pinche cabron*! Eliano. Tell Alfredo to build three pine boxes. Then ride to the ranch and let the Ortegas know what happened. Eliano! Eliano?"

The boy was gone. Hooves shuffled from the stable.

"Boy, if you stole my mule, I'll skin you alive!"

Page kept the paint to a steady, land devouring trot. About five kilometers outside Matalo, he rounded a corner and found Eliano, waiting on the mule. He halted his horse.

"*Chico.* What are you doing here?"

Eliano grinned. "I know a short cut through the hills."

"Yes, but what are you doing here?"

"I want to go with you to *El Norte.* Let me be your *vaquero, Señor* Page. I can already ride and I'll learn how to rope. Oh, *por favor*, please, *Señor* Page."

He looked Eliano over.

"What's your name, boy?"

"Eliano."

"Eliano? No more than that?"

"That's all the name they gave me."

"All right, Eliano. See if you can keep pace. If you reach the river and cross with me, I'll ask Mr. Burrell to hire you as a hand."

"Ah, *muchas gracias, Señor* Page. I'll work hard, I promise."

"I know, *chico.*"

They headed north, toward the Rio Grande and the wild, rugged, Big Bend country.

Eliano sat proud and tall on the mule, fully aware his life as a man had begun.

KILL AND CURE

Robert Lopresti

"I'm sorry," the doctor said. "There's no way we can help you."

Turner sat still, wondering what he was supposed to be feeling. Rage? Disappointment? Despair?

Numb. That's how he felt. Numb.

He swallowed. "Dr. Madison, from what I hear this experiment—"

"Clinical trial."

Turner shrugged. "It's my only hope. Why can't I get in? I know I don't have insurance ..."

It never seemed necessary. He had expected to die young or spend most of his life in prison, getting any treatment he needed on the government's dime. "But I've got plenty of money."

Madison shook her head. She was an attractive African-American woman in her forties, with tightly-curled hair cut short. "There would be no cost to participate in the trial, Mr. Kass. You simply don't qualify."

"Why? I'm too sick?"

"No, you're too young."

Turner blinked. "Excuse me?"

"The protocols for these trials are very precise. They must be in order to get meaningful results. This one is for men between ages forty and fifty. You're only thirty-eight."

He felt his pulse pounding in his ears. "You're saying you won't help me live longer because I'm dying so young? Seriously?"

Dr. Madison's lips tightened. "These trials aren't about individuals. The goal is to determine whether a drug or procedure can assist *categories* of patients. If we can't identify the—"

"Yeah, I get it." He stood up. "Look, there's an easy fix. Forget you saw me. I'll make a new appointment and tell you I'm forty."

"I can't do that."

"You mean you won't. I'm gonna die because of your stupid rule."

Her left hand was under the desk. Do doctors have panic buttons? He couldn't afford a run-in with the cops. Not a man like—

An idea popped into his head, one so crazy he could hardly believe it was there.

He sat down and smiled. Crossing his legs, casual as you please, willing her hand away from the desk. "Look, if I can't change your mind, maybe we can barter."

She frowned. "I don't know what you mean."

"I've got a talent, a skill you might have a use for." Turner felt giddy. Thirteen years in the business, he'd never told anyone this, not a lover, not his brother, not the lawyer who got him off after a little bad luck in Fresno years ago.

Desperate times.

"I'm a hit man."

The doctor stared at him blankly. Then her eyes widened. "You mean—you kill people?"

Turner nodded. "For pay. Exactly."

"And you think I might want someone killed? Is that what you're saying?" She seemed torn between astonishment and fury.

"Look, don't take it personally. I'm playing the only card left in my hand. Besides, several of my customers have been doctors. They had a crooked partner, a cheating spouse ..."

Madison frowned. "My partners are fine, thank you very much. My ex-husband is someone else's problem. And I bitterly resent that you—"

Her face went blank.

Bingo. He said nothing.

It took almost a minute before the doctor focused on him again. "You really are a hitman?"

"It's not something people lie about."

"I mean—" Her hand fluttered. "Do you have any proof?"

"I don't have a union card and I'm not much of a scrapbooker." He smiled. "Tell you what. Give me a name and if there isn't a funeral by the end of the week, you can leave me out of your study."

The doctor faded back into silence. Turner counted out three minutes this time.

"There is someone I ... Someone."

He nodded.

Madison lifted a framed photo off her desk. She gazed at it for a long moment before holding it out.

Turner saw a young Black man wearing a sports coat, a tie, and a big grin. The resemblance was unmistakable.

"Is this who you want me to—"

"No!" She held out her hand and he gave the picture back. For a moment he thought she was going to wipe it off, as if he had sullied it. "That's my son Daniel. He was murdered seven months ago."

Turner nodded again. "So my target is the killer?"

"Yes." Her lips were tight. "You ... eliminate him and I'll sneak you into the study, even if it costs me my license."

"We won't let that happen. Who is the killer?"

"I have no idea."

Daniel Madison was twenty-one years old when he died, a senior in the engineering college at the nearby university. On a Saturday night in October he left campus after dinner in his Subaru Impreza. Sunday morning his body was found beached at the edge of the Wallis River, just outside Harrington, a small city half an hour away. His car turned up at a nearby mall.

The coroner concluded that the facial abrasions were pre-mortem. Someone had beaten him. The fatal blow was a blunt strike at the base of his skull.

"And the cops don't know how it happened?" Turner asked.

Madison looked grim. "So they say."

Turner felt beads of sweat on his forehead. That was usually the first warning that a wave of pain was arriving.

"My memory is that there aren't a lot of Black people in Harrington. It's surprising nobody saw your son."

"Maybe they did."

Turner pressed a hand hard on his abdomen. Sometimes that eased the agony. Not this time.

"You mean, maybe someone killed Daniel because he was Black."

Madison's eyes narrowed. "Would you be surprised?"

"No."

"The cops have any theories as to what happened?"

"Naturally. A drug deal gone bad." Her tone was scornful. "My son did not use drugs. Ever."

Turner figured mothers said that a lot, and were often wrong. But would a student at a big university need to travel to another city for a fix?

"I'll see what I can find out."

"How will you investigate?"

"I have no clue." Turner fought the urge to fold over, curl around the pain in his gut. "Usually by the time I'm called in my clients know too damned much about the targets. But first, let's get me signed up for your study."

"That's not how this is going to work. I need results in advance."

Turner frowned. "You serious? You'd say that to a man who could just kill you?"

"Over the years I've discovered that a lot of men could kill me, Mr. Kass. How would doing that help you?"

He had known mobsters who couldn't match her cool.

Daniel's murder didn't rate much news coverage, but one big-mouth cop spoke to a reporter, and the reporter had passed details on to the doctor.

The police knew Daniel was buying drugs because they had filmed the action at the corner of Rose and Baron Streets for a week, prepping for a big drug bust. The prosecution never happened—the reporter guessed that either the dealer turned out to be too small to bother with or somebody got a walk in return for naming a higher up—but they had film of Daniel Madison buying.

"Although the policeman never saw the supposed film," the doctor noted with a sniff.

So the cops figured Daniel died because of a drug deal, but hadn't looked much further than that. Would that have happened if Daniel was White? Turner didn't know.

If he was the mayor's son? That one was easy.

Turner took the highway from the university to Harrington, using the same exit Daniel would have used. It was a quick trip past a cheerful if struggling downtown to the dubious area around Rose and Baron.

There were three kids selling drugs, not exactly being superspies about it.

They were all White. The tallest of them had tattooed hands and was probably the only one who could drink legally. He was the one who approached cars as they cruised by.

A redheaded boy—maybe sixteen?—appeared and disappeared on signals from his boss. He was the runner, going to a hidden stash to fetch whatever merchandise the customer wanted.

A girl with hair the color and apparent consistency of cotton candy completed the team. She was the lookout, watching the boss's back.

Turner pulled up slowly, following the routine of other customers. The tall one came forward. He was looking over his shoulders, twitching as if he had been sampling his product.

"Whatcha need?"

Turner held out a photo of Daniel Madison and an engraving of Benjamin Franklin. "Information. Did you see this guy back in October?"

"October!" The kid stared at him. "You know how many customers I get in a day?"

"How many Black ones?" Turner asked. "How many who get killed just after buying your stuff?"

"Goddamnit. I ain't the Internet. You're scaring off customers." He reached behind his back. "Either you get out of—Jesus!"

Turner's SIG Sauer was pointed at the kid's head. "Hands in sight on three or die on four. One two three—"

"Okay! Okay!" His tattooed hands were up and open. "You're out of your mind, dude. I don't remember who bought from me last week much last year."

"He didn't buy." It was the girl with cotton candy hair. "The brother was, like you, wanting info. Wack Street."

Turner frowned. "If that's an insult you'll have to explain it."

She rolled her eyes. "It's geography. He though he wanted Wax Street, which is just over there." She pointed west. "The GIS sent him there but all he found at the address were factories. I told him he probably wanted Wack, over on the North Side."

The tattooed one frowned. "How do you know this crap?"

"Wack Street. It's funny." She nodded. "Your friend was going to a party."

"He told you that?"

She shook the cotton candy. "He had a case of Coors on the back seat, and a giant bag of Cheetos. What would you say?"

"Party time." Turner peeled off another hundred. "You pay attention. Why is your friend running the show?"

The gray eyes drilled into his. "You know what a cat's paw is?"

"Yes."

"I don't," said the tattooed one.

She shrugged and headed back to her station.

Turner went west to Wax Street and made a note of the addresses where there were factories. Basically that was the 3000 to 3800 blocks. Which meant the doctor's son had probably been looking for that section of Wack Street.

He returned to the highway—waving at the cotton candy girl—and let the GIS steer him to 3000 Wack Street. It turned out to be in a residential neighborhood full of nice older homes, two story colonials and Tudors.

He pulled over to the curb and sat tapping the steering wheel. How the hell was he supposed to guess which of these joints had hosted a party back in October? This was miles beyond his skill set.

Turner called the doctor. He had purchased two burner phones and given her one. "It protects me too," he had explained. "If something goes sideways I don't want a link to someone with a motive."

He didn't add that murder-for-hire was a death penalty offense.

When she answered he asked: "Did your son know anyone who lived on Wack Street in Harrington?"

"I don't think he knew anyone in that whole wretched town. Maybe there were students from the university living there?"

"Maybe. But I can't break into the school's files and find out who was—" He paused.

"You've got something?"

"Could be. I'll call you back."

Turner opened the trunk where he kept a number of items that came in handy when reconnoitering. He removed a reflective vest, a clipboard, and a name tag with his picture on it. Time to ring doorbells.

Most houses he reached were empty. The two people he did speak to were wary to the point of hostility—why didn't people trust each other anymore?—until on the 3300 block he met an overweight man wearing a bright yellow sweat suit.

He looked like a bearded lemon.

"I'm the noise abatement officer," Turner said. "Following up on some complaints about loud parties."

The lemon raised an eyebrow. "I don't believe it! I phoned last summer and now you show up?"

"We have quite a backlog. Are you still experiencing the problem?"

"No! They shut up last fall. I thought you guys finally did your job."

"I'm glad things improved. Can you tell me when things quieted down?"

He tugged his beard. "It must have been October, because I remember expecting they would keep me up all night on Halloween and instead it was quiet as the dead."

He grinned. "Dead on Halloween. Get it?"

"Did the, uh, complainees move out?"

"Who can tell? Those college brats have been rotating in and out for years. One has more nose rings and the next has more tattoos. That's the only way to tell them apart."

Turner was beginning to feel like a Goddamned detective. "Which house was it, sir?"

The lemon frowned. "Why don't you know that?"

Good question. "To tell the truth, the clerk entered your information wrong. That's one reason for the delay."

"Typical. My tax dollars at work. It's that dump across the street."

A three-story colonial, not as well kept as some of its neighbors.

"Thank you, sir. I'll go talk to them."

"Don't get them started again, for God's sake," the lemon yelled. "And hey, civil servant! Remember your three-hour lunch break!"

Turner decided that if he really was a civil servant he would get fired for strangling citizens.

"Yeah?" The college girl who answered the door at the colonial was blonde. She wore a red tube top and what looked like new jeans, although the front of the legs were already sliced up. Why the passion for pre-damaged clothing these days? Just showing off you could afford to buy stuff that wouldn't last a month?

He was too young to be this grouchy. Of course, unless he got into Madison's drug trial, he might not get much older.

Turner showed his name tag. "I'm investigating an incident that happened here in October."

"Well, don't look at me," she said, looking at him. "I moved in for the spring semester."

"I see."

"Yeah, I had this cool place just off campus, right? But my roommate was bipolar. She decided it was my job to keep her on her meds."

"That's too bad."

"I didn't come to college to play nurse, right?"

"Look," said Turner. "Is there someone here who *could* help me?"

She wrinkled her nose. "Sure! Ali. I'll go get him." She shut the door, then popped it open. "Wanna come in?"

The hallway had seen harder times than the exterior. Each wall was painted a different color, not recently, and there were recycling bins full of beer cans and bottles. From the smell, no one had come to college to play housemaid either.

"Can I help you?"

Ali was not what Turner had expected, given that name. He was short and had the olive skin of the Middle East, but he wore a gallon of hair gel and a nose ring.

"My name is Sam Kass," said Turner. "I'm looking into a party you had here back in October."

The olive skin paled. *Sure as hell something had happened that night.* "Who are you working for?"

Turner shrugged. "I'm just an interested person. But I can call in people with badges if you prefer."

Ali seemed to shrink. He turned around and saw the blonde staring at them.

"Come in. Let's talk in back."

The house had a yard with a raised garden bed.

When Ali was sure they were alone he asked: "What do you want to know?"

Turner showed a photo of Daniel. "Let's start with this guy."

Ali didn't seem surprised. "I don't know what happened to him."

"Oh, man." Turner grinned. "I hope you don't play poker."

"Why?"

"Because you can't bluff to save your life. That may be the worst answer you could possibly dream up."

"What do you mean?"

"You could have said, I don't recognize him. You could have said, he wasn't at the party. But instead you just told me he *was* here. And you know he died that night."

Ali's eyes were wide. "I didn't say anything like that!"

"No? Then what did you mean you don't know what happened to him?"

"I mean after he left the party."

"I didn't ask that. Tell me how he got invited."

"Don't know. He was a stranger, and not the only one. You know what college parties are like. People just show up."

Turner nodded. "Okay. What happened to him after he showed up?"

Ali looked angry. "It's not what happened to him you should be looking at. It's what he did."

"And what's that?"

"He raped a girl."

"That's insane," said Dr. Madison. They were meeting at a bar four miles from her office. "First the police claim he bought drugs and now this Indian—"

"Pakistani-American."

"Whatever! Accuses him of rape. What else? Maybe Daniel sold our nuclear codes to the Chinese."

"If you can't quiet down I'm walking out."

Madison raised her ginger ale with shaking hands. "All right. What's your next move?"

"I have to find a current address for Jennifer Feliz."

"Is she the—" Madison swallowed. "She claims my son—"

"No. She drove the victim to the hospital afterwards."

"I'm coming with you."

"We shouldn't be seen together. Let me—"

"I'm coming *with you*." Her voice rose. "You need a woman for this part."

Which made sense. "Okay. I'll work on getting the address."

The Web made that easy, but they couldn't proceed the next day. Turner woke up in a cold sweat, in so much agony he could barely pick up the phone and call her.

"Do you need to go to the hospital?"

"What can they do for me? You've got the only treatment in town. How about you slip me some of your magic formula?"

"It's under lock and key. Besides, it's not a miracle cure. We're talking about progress over months."

"So you can't help me through this day either."

"Pain medication." She sounded exasperated. "The hospital can monitor your condition. They—"

"Will that help me become your lab rat?"

"No."

"Then I'm not interested. Besides, I picked up pain killers from some free-lance pharmacists downtown. They'll do me fine."

"You shouldn't be self-medicating—"

"See you in the morning, Doc."

He closed his eyes and tried to keep his mind off the agony. Unexpectedly, what came to mind were the faces of people he killed. None of them had suffered like this, although he didn't suppose they would be sympathetic. *Serves you right,* would be more like it.

Turner popped some pills and tried to sleep.

Jennifer Feliz was pretty, Hispanic, and barely five feet tall. She let them into her apartment near the campus but she didn't make them welcome.

"I'm speaking under protest. We shouldn't be having this conversation at all."

Madison frowned. "Then why are you talking to us?"

Feliz folded her arms. "Because your friend here threatened to raise a stink. Call the cops, talk to the university. Violate the victim's privacy. Trust me, she's been through enough."

The doctor nodded. "I don't want to hurt her. But we have to know the truth."

"Why? Who are you two anyway?"

"We're concerned about what happened to your friend," said Turner. "You said Daniel Madison assaulted her."

Feliz's eyes went wide. "What? That's crazy. Who told you that?"

The doctor went limp. "Oh, thank God. I need to sit down." She slumped onto a couch.

Feliz stared from one to the other. "What's going on?"

Turner gestured. "This is Daniel's mother."

"Oh." She sat down on the couch and took Madison's hands. "I thought everyone knew. Your son was a hero."

The doctor swallowed. "You mean Daniel didn't hurt that girl?"

"No! He saved her."

And then they were crying in each other's arms.

The story was a mess because Nora—which is what Jennifer Feliz called the victim— had been a mess when she told it.

Feliz had been invited to the party by Mickey Soames, a cute guy who worked at the gym. She brought her friend Nora along.

The two got separated. An hour later Feliz, who was in the kitchen, heard shouting upstairs.

"I thought I heard Nora's voice. I went up and saw people crowded around the door. Nora was on the bed, naked. I made everyone leave."

Nora told her she had been talking to Soames and a friend of his whose name she never got. The next thing she knew she was on the bed and one of them was on top of her.

"A date rape drug," said Madison.

Feliz glared at her. "Obviously. And before you ask, she wasn't drinking."

She shook her head. "I should have had her back. Instead I was in the kitchen showing someone my recipe for sangria."

"Not your fault."

"No? I brought her to the party. Had to show off my college friends to a girl who was too scared of ICE to go to college."

"What happened next?" asked Turner.

"Nora told me a Black guy—that had to be your son, he was the only Black man at the party—pulled a man off her."

"And then?"

"Nora heard fighting and saw Mickey fall down. Your son chased the other guy out of the room. Mickey got up and followed."

Ali and one of the other guys who were living in the house wanted to call the cops, but Feliz told them not to.

"Nora and her family are all undocumented, you know? She was terrified ICE would deport them and it would be her fault.

"I got her dressed and took her to a hospital emergency room. Gave them a false name."

Turner nodded. "And she wouldn't press charges."

"She didn't dare."

"And what happened to my son?" asked Madison. Her voice quavered.

Feliz shrugged. "I don't know. I took Nora to her parents and didn't get back to town for a week. Otherwise I would have gone to the funeral. I am so sorry about Daniel, but I don't know anything about his death. Are you sure it was related to what happened to Nora?"

The doctor's eyes were slits. "What are you saying? That my son did something *else* that night that got him killed?"

"No, I just ... I'm sorry. I don't know what I meant."

Turner had a pad of paper. "Do us a favor. Write down the names of everyone you know who was there that night."

He convinced the doctor to go back to work. But after the third interview with a party-goer he had to call her. She didn't respond to the burner so he took a break in a city park, watching young women exercising and trying to keep his mind off the pain in his gut.

Turner found himself thinking about Florida. He had stored most of his money there, even bought a house. His retirement plan, vague as it had been, was to move there someday. Would he ever see it again?

He had never made a will. Didn't seem like a good idea to leave a paper trail. But it looked like he would be leaving a lot of money behind. His brother would wind up with college money for his kids.

Do one good deed, anyway.

Daniel Madison had tried to do a good deed, and look how that turned out. The only Black man at the party, the classic stranger in town. Dead in the river.

The burner phone rang.

"I know some more," he told Madison. "It's all bad news."

She laughed, brief and harsh. "What else is new? Tell me."

"We'd better meet." He named another bar.

There was something different about Madison's face when she walked in. Harder, he thought. A warrior in armor ready to face whatever the world threw at her.

She seemed startled when the waitress asked her for an order. She chose mineral water.

"Have you found this Mickey Soames? You have to get him to tell you who the other rapist was—"

"He's dead."

A pause. "You—already?"

"No. Soames died in December. About six weeks after your son. A one-car accident late on a Saturday night."

"Was he drunk?"

"The news doesn't mention booze. It's not like I've seen the coroner's report." He took a breath. "It could have been suicide. You know, remorse."

"Remorse." She said it with scorn. "Do you think people like that feel remorse?"

Funny question to ask me. "I gave up a long time ago trying to guess what people are capable of. You want me to keep looking?"

"What?" It took her a moment to pull herself out of whatever zone she was in. "Of course. We still don't know who killed Daniel."

"You're the boss, Doc."

The interviews became repetitive. Boring. Most of the party-goers had heard that Daniel was a rapist and assumed that his death was related to that somehow.

"People like that," said one girl he talked to in a dorm, "they get into a lot of fights, don't they?"

"People like what?"

She squirmed. "I'm not a bigot."

"Of course not," said Turner. "But what about the party? Was there anyone there who isn't like you? Who had problems with Black people?"

"I don't hang around with racists!"

"Okay. Let's take a different approach. Somebody bashed Daniel Madison on the back of the head. Did you see anyone with blood on their clothes?"

"No, but Mickey must have."

Damn it. Back to the dead man. "Why do you say that?"

"Because Jimmy Biriani complained that he got Mickey a spare shirt from his car, and never got it back."

No one had mentioned Jimmy Biriani before, perhaps forgotten because he had only been at the university for one semester, not returning after Christmas break. But the girl had seen him working as a barista at a coffee shop outside Harrington.

Turner saw the kid with the *Jimmy* nametag as soon as he walked into the shop. He was skinny and had spiked hair with silver highlights. Seemed friendly, chatting with the customers.

When no one was waiting at the counter Turner walked up.

"What can I get started for you?"

"Did you kill Daniel Madison?"

Jimmy Biriani backed up like he'd been slapped. "I don't know what you're talking about."

"You don't want—Goddamn it!"

The kid was running toward the back of the store.

Turner pushed past two astonished customers and raced around the counter. He saw Biriani at the far end of a long corridor. He ran and immediately the pain started again, burning through his abdomen as if he'd just done a marathon. His legs would barely hold him up.

Somehow he made it down the corridor and saw Biriani getting into a Toyota in the parking lot. *Oh no you don't.*

He had his gun out. He thought he would have to shoot out a tire or two and deal with the consequences when a crowd gathered, but Biriani must have had trouble with his keys because Turner got there before he could start the car.

The passenger side door was locked so Turner swung his gun at it. The kid jerked back and dropped his keys.

On the third contact the butt of the gun smashed the window. Turner pointed the gun through it. "Open the door, you bastard, or I'll shoot you in the crotch."

Biriani unlocked the door. Turner got in and tried to brush the shattered glass onto the floor, which only earned him a handful of splinters.

"Damn it. Drive."

"Where?"

"Away. I'll tell you when to stop."

"Please! I didn't do any—"

Turner transferred the gun to his bleeding hand and hit the kid on the ear with the palm of his other hand.

"Ow!"

"Drive."

They parked at the edge of a shopping mall, the one where Daniel's car had been found. Apparently no one at the coffee shop had called 911, because Turner heard no sirens rushing to the rescue.

He had one hand folded over his gut, trying to look like he had the strength to chase Biriani if the kid made a run for it. At least the gun looked pretty healthy.

"I swear to God, mister, I don't know what happened to that guy."

"Sure. That's why you ran when I mentioned his name." He sighed. "Look, Jimmy. Next time you lie or evade I break a finger. I'll run out of patience before you run out of fingers. That's when I decide you're too much trouble and go on to the next name on my list."

There were no more names, but Biriani didn't know that.

"Damn it." The kid banged his fist on the steering wheel. "Goddamn Mickey Soames! It's all his fault."

That name again. "What did he do?"

"It was at the party at Ali's house, you know? I was smoking a joint in the back garden and Mickey came out, asked if we saw a Black dude run by. We had. Ron thought he had been chasing somebody, but I didn't see that."

"Who's Ron?"

"Ron Stein. He was a buddy of mine from high school. I brought him to the party." He shook his head. "Haven't seen him since. Can't blame him."

"So then what happened?"

Biriani swallowed hard. "Mickey told us the Black guy had raped a girl at the party. We ran after him. Found him a block away getting into his car."

He stopped.

"Go on."

"Ron and I—we thought we were just gonna grab him and hold him for the cops but Mickey threw him to the ground and slammed his head in the street. Started kicking him. Jesus."

"You and Ron helped."

"At first. We stopped when it looked like Mickey was gonna kill him."

"But you didn't stop Mickey."

"No." The kid was crying now. "No, we should have. Even if he was a rapist that shouldn't have happened to him."

"He wasn't."

"What?"

"Soames was the one who attacked the girl. He killed Madison so he couldn't tell."

Biriani's eyes went wide. "Oh my God."

Then he got sick.

"I know where you work," said Turner before he left the car. "And since I've got your driver's license I know where you live. If you try to disappear I'll take that as a personal insult. You know what I'll do then?"

Biriani looked at him, wide-eyed. "What's going to happen to me?"

"Life, for a while." He pressed a handkerchief against his bleeding hand. "Death, eventually."

Turner got a Lyft back to the coffee shop and drove away in his own car. He called Madison and two hours later she met him near the edge of a ballfield fifteen minutes from the doctor's office. She sat in the passenger seat and listened without a word as he told her what he had learned.

"So what's the verdict?"

Madison turned to face him, seeming to have trouble focusing. "Verdict?"

"Who do I have to kill to earn my place in your study? Soames is dead. There was another rapist but nobody knows who it was."

Turner stretched. "Biriani and his friend thought they were punishing a bad guy. He says Soames killed Daniel and I believe him. Biriani certainly didn't have the stones for it. When they realized he was dead, Mickey transported your son's body to the river in Daniel's car, with the other two following in his Toyota."

He shrugged. "I'll snuff Biriani and Stein if you want. I don't usually do two-for-one deals, but you've got me over a barrel."

"I don't—" She stopped. She was shaking a little and Turner worried that she might start to cry.

She pulled it together. "I don't want those two dead. I want them in jail."

"Not hard. I'll phone the police tonight."

"What if they won't act on an anonymous tip? After all, they've already decided Daniel died in some drug deal."

"Then I'll call the press and say the cops are covering it up because one of the boys has an uncle on the city council."

"Is that true?"

"Who cares? As soon as somebody—cop or reporter—talks to Biriani he'll crack like an egg. Then it's just a matter of time."

The doctor tapped her hand on the dashboard. "Damn it. This was supposed to give me closure. Get me started on healing."

Turner dug around for something to say. Comforting mourners was a light-year from his job description. "At least Daniel's death wasn't about race. What's so funny?"

Madison was laughing, deep gasping sounds, so hard that she was crying. "Oh my God. If you and I had never met, if we had only emailed or something, I would know right now that you were White."

Turner felt almost embarrassed. "Why is that?"

"Let's reverse it. Let's say Daniel told those White boys that Mickey Soames had raped a woman. Do you think they would have taken his word for it and helped him beat Soames to death?"

"Oh." Turner thought about it. "I see your point."

He paused. "Let's be clear, Doc. I fulfilled my end of the bargain. The fact that you decided you don't want anybody dead doesn't change that. I expect you to get me into that study."

"God." Madison was wiping tears away with the heel of her hand. "I've been so fixated on Daniel I almost forgot."

"What do you mean?"

She took a deep breath. "Look. I'll just say it. There is no study."

Turner squinted at her. "What are you talking about?"

"We cancelled it two days ago. There was a trial going on in Connecticut, different illness but the same drug. It doesn't work."

He frowned. "Okay, screw the study. Get me the meds and I'll take my chances."

"It would be like giving you poison, you understand? We know now they would just make things worse."

He remembered how her tone had been different in the bar. "And you didn't bother to tell me this last night."

Madison ran a hand across her hair. "You were my only chance to find out what happened to Daniel. To avenge him. I figured you'd kill me when you found out about the study, but I was okay with that."

"Jesus. You're crazy."

"I'm a mother who lost her only child."

Turner shook his head. He could feel the pain in his gut starting up again. This was going to be a bad one.

"So what now?" asked Madison. Her hands were folded on her lap, like a little girl ready to take her punishment. "Are you going to kill me?"

Turner waited for the rage to burn, to overcome him. Instead there was numbness, again.

He started the car. "Tell you what, Doc. Go back to your office and try to heal somebody. I'm moving to Florida."

THE RING OF TRUTH

Vicki Weisfeld

Opening night in less than 48 stomach-fluttering hours and the rehearsal for Sweetwater Community Players' new production had come unglued. Set in an ancient Rome ruled by the gods of Farce and Slapstick, *A Funny Thing Happened on the Way to the Forum* presented difficulties that were, our director said, "legion." Chief among them was Kayla Burch, the high school senior playing Philia, the romantic lead.

She kept stepping on the lines of the lead actor, who hoped his Pseudolus would brighten his star in the University of Texas Theater Department and had invited people up from Austin for opening night.

The other actors complained she stood behind them fussing with a prop or shuffling her feet, anxious sounds as distracting as mice scrabbling in the walls. She'd sneak friends backstage. She'd break character and laugh. Amos Franks, our director, got good use out of his lecture on professionalism.

New to this small Texas town, I'd volunteered to stage-manage, thinking I'd meet some interesting people. Possibly Amos took me on in case my job as a reporter for the *Sweetwater Register* would generate extra publicity. Or soften the coverage when the Baptists inevitably protested. Courtesans and cross-dressing were sure to set someone off.

I scheduled rehearsals, arranged costume fittings, and managed our move from the Presbyterian church basement to the Texas Theater for dress rehearsals. Today, I spray-painted walnut-sized wooden rings for three cast members to wear. Seven geese waddled around their carved rims.

Kayla was supposed to wear her ring on a leather thong around her neck, but she was constitutionally incapable of just going along. So here we were, long after the dinner break, and the loose ring on her tiny hand clearly bothered her. I made a note. Amos wouldn't want her fidgeting.

The rehearsal dragged toward an end. The next line was Kayla's.

"How many geese in a giggle?" she asked in her twangy little-girl voice.

"That's 'gaggle,' " I corrected from my second-row seat. We'd run the scene seven times already, and she tripped over that line every time.

"Giggle is funnier," she said.

Amos strode up onto the stage, the sound of his boot heels reverberating through the empty theater. "Philia, honey, your father, Erronius there, has been talking about the rings he gave his missing children, the rings with the *gaggle of geese* on them. Miles, here, is studying his ring. You're looking at yours." He moved close beside her. "Unless all of y'all describe the rings exactly the same way, honey, unless you *all three* say 'gaggle of geese,' our audience will be confused." He bent at the waist to bring his face to hers. "Your line's the key to this whole damn play, sweetheart. On your line, everything changes. It is *not* the time to sow confusion."

Kayla looked to be tearing up or getting mad, hard to say. Not knowing her lines was bad enough, but that night she was so low-energy, she wasn't giving her young lover, Hero—played by her real-life boyfriend Dylan Tower—anything to react to.

The curtain rose on that romantic drama a few weeks before, after Kayla dropped her long-time boyfriend, Lawton Higham. In case she changed her mind, Lawton spent his evenings sitting in his truck outside our rehearsals, listening to country music, revving his engine, and smoking cigarettes.

"Now what's the line? Brianna?" Amos snapped the question at me.

"How many geese in a gaggle," I said.

"Got it, sugar?"

"How many geese in a gaggle," Kayla whispered.

"Fine." The corners of Amos's mouth rose, but he wasn't smiling. He returned to sit beside me.

"I still say giggle is funnier," Kayla said.

"Almighty God," Amos muttered. To her, he said, "I'll sure tell Sondheim, Shevelove, and Gelbart when I see them. Let me think, how many Tonys has this musical won?"

"Seven," I said. "Thirteen, counting revivals."

"Why I keep you around, Yamato," Amos said.

"What kind of crazy word is 'gaggle' anyway?" Kayla twisted the ring.

"Collective noun," I said. "Specific to each animal."

"Like *flock* of sheep," a cast member said.

"*Herd* of cattle."

"*Colony* of bats." Pseudolus twirled his finger beside his ear and pointed to Kayla.

"*Murder* of crows."

"*I* didn't say it," Amos muttered and called out, "We're *so* close to the end, y'all. I've got a cold and frosty Lone Star waiting. Take your places."

The actors shifted around, the musicians smartened up for the finale, and I gave the line to start the scene. When we got to Kayla, she stared at the ring and jerked it off her finger. "How many geese in a ..." She crumpled to her hands and knees. The ring skittered into the orchestra pit, and I jumped up to retrieve it.

"Hellfire!" Amos hurried onstage. His fallen Philia lay on her side, panting. "Brianna!"

"Doctor?" I yelled. I had my phone out as I entered the orchestra pit, saying, "Kayla took off Philia's ring and it fell ..."

"Bounced off my music stand." The second violin pointed.

I started to pick up the ring, but the gold paint looked smeary, and I already had plenty of it on my best jeans and under my fingernails. "Anybody have a tissue?"

The clarinet rummaged in her bag. I took one from her pack, wrapped the ring in it, and shoved it in my front pocket.

"Amos? You want a doctor?" I called from where I stood, eye-level with the stage, waving my phone.

One of the scantily clad courtesans—a nurse in real life—knelt alongside Kayla. "She's not breathing." She pressed her fingers to the side of the girl's throat.

"I'm calling an ambulance!"

The nurse slumped for several beats before tilting her head to meet Amos's eyes. In a hoarse voice, she said, "I think—it's too late. She's—Kayla's dead."

Dylan's howl broke the stunned silence.

Transformed from stage manager to newspaper reporter, I grabbed a pad from my bag and hurried onstage. Everyone talked at once, and the stories were identical. We'd all noticed how pale and shaky Kayla was. We thought she was nervous about opening night or upset by another confrontation with Amos. She hesitated over that troublesome line, wavered a few seconds, then collapsed. We thought she fainted. Meanwhile, the orchestra sat frozen, jaws dropped, the onstage drama way beyond expectations.

My 911 call brought the Sweetwater Police Department, and the evening we thought was near its end had just begun.

In the newsroom I was briefly a minor celebrity. My editor, Charlie, took it easy on me, a witness to death and all. I wanted in on the story of Kayla's death, and he gave me the softball assignment of interviewing family and friends for a profile. I also wrote a short follow-up about her role in the play. Amos was more than generous with his comments, and the cast members were, well, actors playing bereaved colleagues.

I interviewed Kayla's parents and asked about any health problems she had. I was thinking a congenital heart defect or something. Her stepdad didn't say much, but her mother squashed my idea like a blister beetle. "Never sick a day," she said. What with those pesky government confidentiality rules, Kayla's doctor wouldn't confirm that, nor would the school. And because we were still waiting for the medical examiner's report, our news stories were stuck with "unexpected death."

My most interesting interview was with Dylan Tower. In a brief time, he and Kayla had become inseparable, as teenagers do. Two days after her death, over a Dr. Pepper, we talked. I had the impression he felt some guilt, like he'd missed something or hadn't said the right thing.

"She seemed happy with you," I said.

"I *thought* she was. With me, she could forget that other stuff."

"Other stuff?" I wasn't even probing for my story. It was just a natural response.

"Yeah, her family and their shit. Her dad's a psycho. Her mom divorced him, couple years back, and married a guy with two little kids. Kayla was just a babysitter to him. She'd say, 'Why can't he leave me alone?' "

Now my reporter's antennae quivered. "Was he abusive? Did she say?"

"She never said *that*. He was just mean, saying stuff like, 'I can't wait 'til you stop sucking on the family tit.' Stuff like that."

"Harsh."

"Yeah. She hated him. But her real dad was some kind of drug dealer. He took off."

"Wow." The parents hadn't hinted at any of this.

"Kayla was a dead-ringer for her real dad. Every time her mom looked at her she saw her ex. 'And you're another loser, just like him,' she'd say."

"Kayla's last name was Burch. That's her stepdad's name, right?"

"Kayla's mom made him adopt her, so the ex couldn't get her."

"What's the stepdad do?"

"Owns a feed store out near the Interstate."

Kayla, who seemed such a simple soul, had a complicated life. Not that much of Dylan's information would go in my story.

We postponed the play opening, and Amos found a new actor to play Philia. She'd had the role in Albuquerque, and everyone was grateful for the end of off-script theatrics. That intense week of rehearsals helped us get past the tragedy, in the consoling tradition of "the show must go on." Amos dedicated the production to Kayla, and it was a big success. It sure got that extra news coverage.

A week or so later, I was still baffled about Kayla's mysterious death. Actually, I felt I owed her something to atone for my mean thoughts. One afternoon, I found my editor Charlie and Max Reid, the *Register*'s crime reporter, eating lunch at the Triple Joe Café next to our offices. I stopped by their booth with my bag of takeout. Max had solid connections with the medical examiner's office, so I asked, "Any details about Kayla Burch's death yet?"

"Not a damn word," he said around a mouthful of chicken salad, "which is suspicious in itself. If it was heart failure or a burst appendix, we'd know already."

"So, what's the holdup?"

"Toxicology testing. Takes a while."

"Toxicology? They think Kayla was on drugs?"

"Drugs, poison, powerful allergen."

"Allergen?" I asked.

"Peanuts, kiwi."

"Not much kiwi around here." What had Kayla eaten at the cast dinner that night? I hadn't a clue. "Accidental or on purpose?" I persisted. "If on purpose, murder or suicide?"

We obviously couldn't answer any of that. Charlie wiped his mouth with a pile of napkins. "What I'm hearing here is we need open minds. Can y'all do some digging? Without alarming anybody. When we do get the ME report, let's not be starting from scratch. What do you think, Max?"

"Seems wide open to me."

"I could look into some things," I said, "without alarming anybody."

I was at the County-City Library when it opened Saturday morning. My librarian friend, Effie, had lived in Sweetwater so long, she could write Nolan County's history—come to think of it, she had, as past editor of the historical society's newsletter. I brought pecan rolls and coffee, and she swept me into a conference room.

I described the puzzle of Kayla's death and how there should be a story in there—a cautionary tale for other teens, maybe. Surely something beyond "thoughts and prayers." Kayla hadn't been a big library patron, but Effie did know Dylan. "As far as I can tell, he and his friends aren't into the stuff that gets kids in trouble these days.

But what do I know? It's around."

"I see those trainwrecks at the courthouse all the time." I scraped up the last pecan bits from my napkin. "What about Kayla's parents?"

"Don't know them. Her stepfather, Dave Burch, he's a Sweetwater native. His father started the feed business, and Dave took over after he died."

"What do you think of him?"

Effie pursed her lips, a signal she didn't like what she was going to say. "Now, mind, I don't know him well. I *do* know when he started running the business, some of the long-time employees quit, and I stopped buying my garden supplies there. Always new people, not much help."

"Kayla's biological father, I'm told, is or was dealing drugs."

"Oh, Lord. I'm sorry to hear it. Texas drug dealers are mean as rattlers and twice as dangerous."

I left Effie with my thanks and dragged myself home to tackle an afternoon at the laundromat. Among the dirty clothes were my paint-splattered jeans. "Hey, Ruth?" I yelled to my roommate. "How do I get this gold paint out of my new jeans?"

She came in and looked over my shoulder. "Nail polish remover. I'll get mine." I patted the pockets for the tell-tale squish of a forgotten tissue and felt a hard lump. Kayla's ring. I dropped the jeans and sat on the floor next to them.

When Ruth returned with the polish remover, I said, "Can we call Robert?" Sweetwater police officer Robert Torres was married to Ruth's best friend. "I think I've been hiding evidence."

I don't know why I put it that way, and while waiting for Robert, I thought about it. Yes, that ring irritated Kayla. Yes, the paint job looked funny when I saw it in the dimly lit orchestra pit. But when the new Philia arrived, we had three rings. Something didn't make sense. I explained all this to Robert.

"Where's the ring?" he asked.

"Right front pocket. I didn't touch it. You know, in case ..." I let the thought trail off, hoping he'd finish my sentence with some information.

"In case what?" Nope.

"What's strange is that Travis, our props guy, made *three* rings, and we had all three for the show. This one is ..." I shrugged.

"Hmm. Just 'in case,' I'll put it in a plastic bag. Got one?"

Ruth brought a sandwich bag from the kitchen. Once the ring was inside, I held out my hand, "May I?" I shook the bag so the tissue fell away and examined the surface of the ring, the too-crudely carved circle of geese. "There's only six."

"How many should there be?"

"Our gaggles of geese all had seven. This isn't one of the rings from the show."

"You still have the others?"

I called Travis. Yes, he had the rings, and yes, he was at home. Robert would stop by.

A few stubborn flecks of gold wouldn't come out of my jeans, but they met Ruth's Texas standard: "Man on horseback would never notice."

My original interviews with Kayla's best friends had been pretty useless. They were too upset. Now I cycled back to them. Viva—aptly named—was an enthusiastic talker, while Ariana verged on sullen. We chatted, then I got to the meat of it.

"Was Kayla upset about anything?"

"Well, yeah," said Ariana. "Her grandma's dying. The whole family's really upset. She stays in a hospital bed in the family room. Kayla couldn't watch TV or nothin'."

"And something else," Viva said. "Kayla was breaking up with Dylan."

"Really? Why?"

"I never found out why. She just said they couldn't be together any more. Then her stepdad came home and made her stop texting."

I offered some trail mix, apologizing about the peanuts, "in case you're allergic." They weren't, but they knew people allergic to shellfish and tree nuts. They were sure Kayla wasn't.

"She said she might get back with Lawton." Munching trail mix, Viva gave Ariana a poke. "Now you can get another shot at Dylan."

"Not interested." Ariana picked her cuticle.

"You know you are. That's why you messed with her ring. Backstage."

"Shut *up*."

Lawton, Kayla's ex, cold-shouldered me when I ran into him that night at the Southside Grill. The first time I'd tried to talk to him, he slammed the door of his truck in my face, nearly skinning my nose. Now he was with a couple of buddies as gangly and scruffy as he was. I persisted.

"I wrote the story about Kayla Burch's death for the *Register*. So sad. I understand you were close."

"You're the bitch from the theater. You *know* we was close."

Best let that lie. "You and Kayla were getting back together?"

His companions snorted Dr. Pepper. One said, "Hot damn! You been keepin secrets, boy!"

"Yeh? It's a secret from me too then. I did fin'ly talk to her, and she said we should go out to Lake Sweetwater for a picnic one of these times. *Don't* put that in the paper," he pointed a grimy finger at me.

The boys nudged each other and snickered. "Uhhh-uhhh-uh. You know what that means."

"Yeh? Well, nothin' came of it, did it?"

The pimply one said, "Anyways, what the hell did she see in *you*?"

Lawton, red-faced, started to rise out of his seat, and I said, "How long were you and Kayla together?"

"Since eighth grade. On and off. Mostly on." He finally made a glassy eye-contact. "She's the only girlfriend I have ever had and ever will have."

The smart retorts apparently caroming inside his pals made them jounce like two bags of microwave popcorn.

As I walked away, I heard a high-pitched "I'll never love another" and the smack of a fist hitting the table.

When I visited the feed store for a follow-up conversation with David Burch, he greeted me with "Why're you stirring up trouble? She's dead and there's nothin' to be done about it."

"I'm not stirring up anything. I asked whether you have further thoughts about Kayla and the … circumstances of her death."

"You people—" He started to walk away.

"We journalists? Or we twenty-somethings?" If I kept this up, Charlie would have to borrow Amos's professionalism lecture.

He came back and barked in my face. "You Orientals start your wars, let us settle your hash, then leave your crappy countries and move here, to enjoy everything America offers."

Oh boy. I said, "My granddad and his brothers served in the US Army in World War II. You've heard of the Purple Heart battalion? His youngest brother was killed in Korea. And my dad and uncles fought in Vietnam. What was your unit?" I could hear Charlie now.

To break off Burch's death-stare, I said, "Kayla's friends say nice things about her. I just wondered whether you'd noticed any change, anything unusual, before she died."

"No. You people saw more of her than we did those last weeks."

"Oh. We thespians."

A fragrant pot of Ruth's four-alarm chili simmered on the stove. I poured us both a Pacifico and described my encounter with Dave Burch. I held the cold empty to my temple and moaned, "I can't believe I said all that."

"C'mon. Asshole deserved it. Just be glad he's not a big advertiser."

"Holy crap! I didn't think of that."

"Not your job, sweetie." Ruth's chili and my guacamole and chips were our favorite dinner. "Love your guac!" She piled some onto her plate.

"California roots," I said. "We have a feel for the avocado."

She raised a laden chip to her mouth and asked, "What's up with that ring Robert took? That prop thing?"

"It was one Travis roughed out, trying to get the right look. Somebody fished it out of the trash backstage."

"Interesting."

"Kinda. But is it significant?"

Ruth had a look of puzzled concentration, like she was trying to work something out. "Here's a crazy thought," she said.

"Spill."

"Kayla's dad is in the wind, right? But his drug-dealer *compadres* would know he's from Sweetwater, might know about Kayla even."

This train of thought might travel to a lot of interesting places.

"So, what if he made them mad, which is probably not that hard?" Ruth continued. "What if he ran off with their money or drugs or whatever, and they threatened Kayla? And he didn't cooperate, so they carried out their threat."

"That only works if she was murdered."

"Yeah, sure. Course."

We spun scenarios all through dinner. "Maybe they wanted to make Kayla sick to get her dad's attention and overdid it?" I said. "She was tiny. A dose of something a bulked-up ex-con would tolerate could kill her."

"Lord knows they can get their hands on whatever," Ruth said.

About a month after Kayla died, Max finally got the call from the medical examiner's office. "Kayla Burch," he yelled to Charlie and hurried out—unusual for Max, generally regarded as one of the laziest humans Nolan County has ever produced.

"So?" I asked when he approached my desk on his return.

"Overdose," he said and breezed by. "Prescription drugs. Two of 'em."

I was prepared to believe Kayla might have been exposed to some recreational substance, given the Texas-sized parade of drug defendants I saw every Monday in court. But prescription meds?

"Share, OK?" I called after him.

He waved some papers and didn't turn around. I trailed him into Charlie's office. I wanted in on this story.

"Why the delay in reporting?" Charlie asked when Max finished his summary.

"Apparently, the mebalo—"

"Metabolites," I said, before I could stop myself. I started cleaning my glasses with my shirttail as if someone else had prompted him.

"—were funky, because multiple substances were involved. And because exposure was from something she ingested *and* through the skin."

"Weird," I said. "She was wearing her play costume. Lots of people handled it."

Max said, "They identified an"—he gave me an anticipatory dirty look—"or-gan-o-phos-phate on the ring."

"Insecticide," Charlie said. "Real skull-and-crossbones shit."

"Available everywhere," I said, thinking of Dave Burch's business, of Viva's accusation and Ariana's 'Shut up!'

"Not enough to do any damage, though. Oxycodone and alprazolam killed her." He spoke slowly.

"Oxy *and* an anti-anxiety med?" I said. "No wonder she died."

Charlie said, "What this doesn't tell us is, deliberate or accidental? Maybe she was gardening and got the insecticide on herself. But the pills? Hell, I don't know."

I didn't know, either, but I wanted to find out. The more I learned about Kayla and her personal life—her indifferent parents, her jealous friend, her barnacle boyfriends—the worse I felt about how I'd misjudged her.

"What do the cops think?" Charlie asked.

"If they've got any theories, they're not sharing," Max said.

"What's our take then? Suspects?" Charlie asked. "Motive and opportunity?"

In the vacuum created by Max not saying anything, Charlie looked to me.

"Kayla herself, of course. Since it happened, I've found out a lot of upsetting stuff was going on in her life. But suicide just before the play opens?"

"Stranger things have happened," Max said, unhelpfully.

"Who else?" asked Charlie.

I ticked them off. "Jimmy Vick, the lead actor. He was furious with all Kayla's disruptions." I thought about this. "Can't believe that was a strong enough motive, but he might have had opportunity. Lawton Higham, the ex-boyfriend. I don't discount a broken heart, but as far as I know, no opportunity."

Max, apparently cottoning to the broken-heart motive, said, "Those Highams are trouble."

"Dylan Tower, the current boyfriend. Definite opportunity, but puppy dog devoted. Kevin Littlefield, Kayla's biological father, a supposed drug dealer. Motive and opportunity unknown. Ditto his recent whereabouts."

It was Charlie's turn to look interested. "Max, find out what you can about him."

"Littlefield's drug cronies, if you cast that net a little wider. Whoever they are. But what opportunity would they have had?" I asked the air. "Finally, Dave Burch, Kayla's stepdad. Some opportunity, at least given all the pesticides at the feed store, but weak motive. I don't think he cared about Kayla enough to kill her."

"Guilty secret?" Charlie asked.

"They didn't get along, but, according to Dylan, no actual abuse. And he'd know."

Charlie said, "If somebody gets shot, the *hombre* with the rifle can be in the next county. If somebody's given too many pills, the killer is right up next to her. That's where our story is, somewhere close. Clint Tower's boy. Try him again."

On Saturday, I took Dylan to the Southside Grill for a burger. He seemed at loose ends, unfocused, but as always, eager to talk about Kayla. "If Kayla's dad wanted her out, what would happen after graduation?"

He pushed French fries through a pool of ketchup mixed with hot sauce, not really eating them. "She was scared about that, but it didn't stop her sassing him." He grinned, remembering. "She thought she could get a scholarship for college. Between semesters she'd live with friends or her aunt in Big Spring."

"Sounds iffy," I said, poking at a salad.

"Which is why I said we should get married."

"You did?" First I'd heard this.

"Sure. Why not?"

I took that question as rhetorical and didn't answer.

"I wanted to," he said. "She did too, at first. And she would have, except Lawton—"

"—wanted to get back together with her, right?"

"Gave her endless grief." A tear hung on the rim of his eye deciding whether to fall.

"Would she have gone back to him?"

"She loved *me*," he said.

"I suppose her parents wouldn't let her get married."

"They didn't care. It was my parents who tore the roof off. They're set on sending me to UT in Austin, but I said I wouldn't go if Kayla couldn't go with me, which she couldn't. My dad said marrying her was stupid, and only a stupid kid would think of it."

Maybe this was why Kayla felt she had to break up with him. "Did Kayla know how they felt?"

"Hell, yeah. She saw how upset I was. My folks didn't like her at the house, so I was at her place all the time. We talked a lot. I told her it would be the two of us against all of them."

"And?"

"She ran out of the house crying. Maybe she was upset because my parents absolutely didn't like her. 'Don't you go getting that girl pregnant,' my mother hollered. 'Y'all not careful, she'll rope you good and tight.' It was embarrassing." He laid his hands flat on the table to stop their shaking. "I know she called Lawton. I was afraid she'd hurt herself or run away, maybe with him. She wouldn't even let me say the word 'married.' Then she ... died, and ..."

"You've been through a lot."

"Yes, ma'am. I just wanted to keep her from doing something awful. But she was too upset. She wouldn't listen."

At that moment, Robert Torres and his partner walked into the Southside. Dylan looked ready to jump out of his seat.

When they passed our booth, Robert said "Howdy," his eyes never leaving the trembling Dylan.

"Officer Torres, this is Dylan Tower." I introduced myself to his partner, "Brianna Yamato, reporter for *The Register*."

"Angel Ramirez." Ramirez also watched Dylan. "You're the kid whose girlfriend died a few weeks back, right?"

"Yeah." Dylan's throat sounded dry as dust.

They took the empty booth behind us. Dylan started to cry and muttered, "I didn't mean it. She needed to calm down."

What in the world—

"It was an accident. I didn't know—"

This was heading someplace bad. "Dylan, stop talking. Don't say another word. I'm taking you home."

"But I want to explain—"

"Dylan, shut up." I grabbed our check. "Let's go."

Outside, I said, "I don't know what you were going to say in there, but you need to talk to your parents first." I had a damn good idea what it was, and the next day, I called Robert and discovered I was right.

I couldn't stop thinking about Dylan and the terrible decision he made. But mostly, I saw poor bewildered Kayla, a drama queen to the end, staring at a ring with six, not seven geese, and whispering, "How many geese in a gaggle?"

Teen's Death Ruled Accidental Overdose

By Brianna Yamato

Wednesday, October 17—No criminal charges will be filed against Dylan Tower, arrested Saturday night at his home in connection with the death of Kayla Burch, who died last August after collapsing during a play rehearsal. This decision came during a conference yesterday involving county prosecutor Don Hubbard and Tower's attorney Frank Lamar, in which the court ordered Tower to perform three hundred hours of community service.

County medical examiner J.L. Crawford reported Burch died from an overdose of prescription drugs. Lamar acknowledged Tower had surreptitiously administered a small amount of the drugs to the victim, unaware Burch already had taken a much larger amount herself.

Security footage from the restaurant where Tower and Burch had dinner the night she died showed him adding two pills to Burch's soft drink. Tower admitted having taken the pills, a narcotic painkiller and an anti-anxiety medication, from the bedside of Burch's ill grandmother.

However, toxicology tests found a much higher blood-level of the drugs than could be accounted for by the pills Tower provided. A note of apology, found after a renewed search of the dead teen's room, confirmed she'd pilfered a sufficient number of her grandmother's pills for a fatal overdose, Crawford said.

In a statement after the conference, Lamar said, "It was never Dylan's intent to harm Kayla. On the contrary, he thought he was helping her through an emotional rough patch."

Said prosecutor Hubbard, "Dylan Tower's contribution to Kayla Burch's death, if any, was minimal. In the great state of Texas, a manslaughter charge requires a degree of recklessness that, in this case, doesn't exist. My office is convinced this is a rare instance when a trial would simply do more harm than good."

CRACKDOWN

DJ Tyrer

It doesn't say much for the new DA's much-publicised crackdown on crime and thuggery when a fellow gets jumped by two masked thugs in the Hall of Records.

Luckily, I'd just been about to tear out a page from a volume of land records, so was keeping one ear and one eye out for the officious little weasel who ran the place and had snootily told me "this isn't a lending library."

(Why do they always say that? Do they think we don't know?)

So, anyway, I caught a flash of movement down the aisle and wasn't caught *completely* by surprise.

Still, it would've been nice to have enough warning to avoid a numbing blow to my arm. I dropped the book I was holding and they promptly trampled over it.

One of the toughs, a nasty little squirt who could've been the weasel beneath his mask, came at me with a cosh. The other, a big menace, had a pair of brass-knuckles and knew how to use them, giving me a good sock in the gut that was probably going to have me passing blood in the morning.

I staggered back and managed to fend off a couple of blows, but with my right arm as numb as an Irishman on St. Patrick's Day, I knew I was in trouble.

On the positive side of the balance sheet, the pair had blown their big advantage. If one had come at me from either end of the aisle, I would've been done, trapped between the ceiling-high shelves. Instead, they'd come together like a couple of schoolkids partnered up on an outing, squandering their advantage and getting in each other's way in the narrow space.

So, I was able to fall back and avoid the worst of it, until I had the chance to snatch one of the land-registry books off the shelf.

Now, when I say 'book,' you're probably thinking of a large hardback novel, maybe even a good-size atlas, but you're still thinking too small. These things are huge, the size of a coffee-table's top and a couple of inches thick, heavy as hell.

The book made a good shield, absorbing a good few blows, and, my arm having regained some feeling, I was able to raise it up over my head and bring it down—

smack!—on the little squirt's, crumpling him to the floor with a sound like a deflating bagpipe. I hoped it *was* the weasel—he'd clearly sold me out.

The big guy paused, clearly not sure how to react, so I jabbed him in the gut with the book, doubling him up, then chucked it, turned and ran.

It would've been nice to have gotten the property details, but somebody clearly didn't want me to and who was I to argue against such a polite request?

I headed back to my office to have a couple of shots of 'medicine' and ponder what I knew so far.

Big Daddy Escovar, the richest man in the city, was dead and though the police said it was an accident, his widow wasn't convinced he'd choked on a piece of shrimp; not when he hated seafood.

She'd hired me to investigate his death, something the cops were showing no interest in, despite all the new DA's big talk.

Big Daddy Escovar had been about to sign a deal on some property on the east side of town, where the cattle-pens used to be, back when the city was a beef hub. An area of empty lots and slum dwellings, it wasn't worth a bean, and I'm certain the police hadn't paid it any heed. But, a little digging told me that the interstate was coming our way and would terminate right there. Whoever owned that area was bound to make a killing when it returned to life.

Instead, it was a murder. A little more digging revealed several more deaths, all associated with the route of the planned interstate. Looking for who'd purchased the land from the estates of the deceased was why I'd been at the Hall of Records: Follow the money, as the number one maxim of the gumshoe's creed has it.

Although I didn't have the list, I could recall some of the names because I knew them from the obituaries column of the city paper, local low-lives whose careers had been ended in a variety of interesting ways, such as Micky Goodman, a bad boy who'd wound up in a ditch with his throat slit. It would be one hell of a coincidence if a cavalcade of folks who shared the names of dead crooks happened to be buying property shortly after their namesakes' deaths. No, their names were being used for someone else's seedy ambition.

But, was someone skimming the obits like me, or were they offing the petty crooks in order to use their identities?

In other words, just how nasty a conspiracy had I stumbled upon? One that was happy to stick with coshes and brass-knuckles, or one that would kill to keep its secrets?

I finished my bottle of 'medicine' and sent my secretary down to the local bodega to buy some more. I had a feeling it was going to be one of those cases …

Tipping my chair back against the wall, I enjoyed the warm glow that was spreading through my body and tried not to think of the danger, just my next move.

The problem was, I hadn't a clue what to do next. I mean, I had the conspiracy nailed down in my own mind, but I didn't have a single piece of evidence worth a plug nickel to take to the police. Look, I know Lieutenant Delgardo from back when we were pounding the beat together and the man has no imagination. He'd happily assume Micky Goodman's virtuous doppelgänger, and the sweet namesakes of a dozen other hoodlums, were buying up property along the route of the planned interstate and all was well with the world. Without something solid to shake him up, I was stuck.

But, who was behind it? About the only thing I did know was that Big Daddy hadn't been a part of it, although he'd probably had much the same idea the conspirators did …

Which left any number of wealthy investors lacking in morals and mobsters looking to launder their money through property, both local and out-of-town.

So, I decided to go have a word with the coroner. The police might've written off Big Daddy's death as a tragedy, but maybe the coroner had found something that could tell me more.

Doctor Sommers was busy tucking into a bloody steak when I arrived at his office. There's something very odd about a man who insists on eating his lunch at the autopsy table and uses a scalpel in place of a knife and fork, but he's always happy to discuss his 'patients,' as he calls them, so I couldn't really complain.

"Big Daddy Escovar," I said.

"Just done him." He stabbed his blade into his steak like a stone-cold killer sticking his victim. "Interesting."

"Interesting? How?"

"He had a piece of shrimp lodged deep in his windpipe, but he'd also ingested a lethal dose of caffeine."

"Caffeine, as found in a regular cup of joe?"

"Yep."

"It's poisonous?" Sometimes, you had to wonder if anything in this world is actually safe.

Sommers gave a nod and popped some more bloody steak into his mouth and chewed.

"You know how, if you drink lots of coffee to keep yourself awake, you can get a bit jittery, heart hammering, right."

"Sure." I knew that feeling well from long, lonely nights staking out some target to catch them breaking their marriage vows like a cheap vase. Reminds you that you're still alive.

"Well," said Sommers, "you drink enough coffee, I mean gallons of the stuff, and your heart doesn't just hammer, it goes—" He smacked his hands together with a clap like a gunshot; I winced.

"So, you're saying he died from caffeine?"

"Hard to say. But, if he hadn't choked, he was a goner anyway. Might've choked because his heart gave out as he was about to swallow."

"That's hardly likely," I told him. "His widow says he never touched seafood. Tell me, could he have drunk that much caffeine by accident?"

Sommers laughed and spat out some partially-chewed meat. "Maybe, but even a serious coffee addict would be hard pressed to drink that much. Not that I found more than a mug in his stomach. The DA wants me to put down accidental death, but," he shrugged, "it's one hell of an accident!"

One hell of an accident indeed! A man who, I knew, was more partial to sangria or a good wine, drinks enough coffee to float a battleship *and* suddenly decides he'd like to try some shrimp, despite hating the stuff? You might as well suggest the Grand Wizard of the Klan take up Catholicism and wed the granddaughter of a slave.

The new DA might not want to hear it, but this was murder in my book, no doubt about it.

But, why caffeine? It seemed a cockamamie way to kill someone. Still, it was the only lead I had.

Okay, so who's awash with caffeine? My first thought was coffee wholesalers, but Sommers said that Big Daddy's stomach had had no more than a mug's worth of coffee in it. And, while I could imagine holding down a dying man to shove a shrimp down his throat or perhaps sticking one in after death, the idea they stuck a funnel in his mouth and poured a gallon of coffee into him was just ludicrous.

Not coffee, then. Something else. But, what? What else was there that used a lot of caffeine?

Then, it struck me: Cola.

Coca Cola. Pepsi Cola. Doc Strong's Patented Pep-up Cola. They were all advertised on the strength of their caffeine. On a hot summer's night, of which we have more than our fair share, a few bottles of cola can do the job where a steaming mug of coffee is too much to face.

Doc Strong's Patented Pep-up Cola was the only brand brewed locally, so it was the place to start looking. They had to have plenty of caffeine on site, in addition to whatever else went into their secret recipe. (I'd heard refined monkey glands, but that was probably just a rumour.)

I drove out to the bottling plant that evening, parked some distance away behind a sign advertising a new housing development. There'd be a night-watchman, of course, but I hoped I could avoid him and poke about.

The bottling plant was just as you'd expect, full of vats and pipes and store rooms with sacks and jars in them. The secret recipe was, doubtless, locked away in a safe, but that wasn't what I was after. I was looking for details of their employees, owners and investors, anything I could tie to the dodgy land deals.

Well, I certainly found something: Mickey Goodman and numerous other low-lives were listed in their register of employees. Delgardo, I'm sure, would be naive enough to assume this was nothing more than another coincidence, but it was practically a smoking gun to my eyes, or a handy vat of caffeine.

Then, came the clincher.

Unfortunately, I barely had more than a moment to take it in before the night-watchman found me and I found out that he wasn't alone, but had a couple more goons with him.

Even more than the Hall of Records, they clearly didn't want me poking my nose in.

The night-watchman was an old guy with a gammy leg who slumped on a crutch, which he used it to wallop me in the crotch, while the two goons, big guys, seized hold of my arms.

"You whopped me earlier," one said, socking me in the gut to ensure I'd be passing blood for a week; "should've kept your nose clean."

Though he was in a suit and tie, now, it was clear he was the tough from the Hall of Records.

"You keep sticking your nose in," the other said, popping out the blade of a flick-knife, "and, you're going to lose it, buddy."

He nicked my cheek as a friendly reminder.

"Dammit, that hurts," I said as they dragged me through the bottling plant to the front gate and I groped for my ankle holster. They tossed me out onto the road.

"Next time, you—oh, hell!"

I shot out the big guy's knee.

The other hood tossed the knife and held up his hands, while the night-watchman tossed aside his crutch and miraculously regained the ability to run.

"Handy," I said. "You'll be needing that."

The man sobbed and writhed on the ground.

"Not so tough, now, eh? The moral of the story is: Don't forget to pat someone down *before* you lay about them, schmuck."

Only, my story wasn't quite over and I high-tailed it to my car and back towards town.

I knew who was behind it all.

Doc Strong's Patented Pep-up Cola Company's sole shareholder: Daniel Bamford, our new District Attorney …

No wonder he wanted Sommers to rule Big Daddy's death an accident. Hell, even his crackdown on crime seemed nothing more than a means to supply a slew of deceased low-lives to list as property owners.

What was it with our DAs? When they weren't in the pay of crooks, they were crooks themselves!

Besides posing a philosophical conundrum, it also raised the question of: How the hell do you go after the man in charge of prosecuting crime?

I guess you call in the G-men and they hand the case to a federal prosecutor, but how could I persuade them to intervene? As with Delgardo, I didn't have the hard evidence and, in my experience, G-men were just as hidebound and lacking in imagination.

My attempts to formulate a plan were cut short when I realised a couple of cars were coming up fast on my tail and, behind the glare of their headlights, I could see they each had a guy with a tommy-gun on both running boards.

Maybe I shouldn't have shot the schmuck's knee out, but we'd clearly crossed a line now. No more fun and games and brass-knuckles, these guys meant business.

They ventilated the rear of my ride and I was pretty damn lucky they didn't ventilate me.

I could see the morning's headlines now, the DA using my death as an example of just how important it was for all right-thinking citizens to back his initiative. Gee, it gave me a lump in my throat, like vomit, to think I could be so helpful.

If I were a Hollywood actor, I would've steered with one hand and returned fire with the other. But, I'm not, so I killed my lights and put my foot down and prayed loud and fast as I took a winding road into the hills, hoping to lose them.

When I was confident their high-beams were far enough behind me, I swung off the road and into a small orange grove. Thankfully, they sped past and I knew I'd make it alive till sun-up.

I needed a place to hole up for a while, so headed to Stan Leibowitz's place. I'd solved the murder of Stan's sister, Joyce, but he just didn't have the cash to pay me off: A dollar here, ten cents there, plenty more to come. I was going to offer him a chance to knock a lump sum off what he owed.

"Twenty bucks off your debt if you can hide me till evening," I said and he nodded happily.

We covered my car with a tarpaulin in his backyard and I was grateful for a chance to sleep.

There was nothing to connect him and me, even my secretary only knew him as a deadbeat who owed me money, and nobody came snooping around.

Stan's wife is a seamstress and was able to stitch my cheek up, in addition to serving some tasty pretzels for lunch.

I hid there till evening, then borrowed Stan's beat-up old van—another five bucks paid off—and drove for City Hall, where the radio said the DA was holding a gala for the great and the good to celebrate a 'new dawn' for the city, one in which, doubtless, he'd be raking it in.

Along the way, I paused at a payphone to call Big Daddy's widow and make sure she'd be in attendance. I couldn't guarantee she'd see justice done in a court of law, but I could ensure she saw justice done in some form.

The valet wasn't too impressed when I pulled up in front of City Hall in Stan's old truck.

"Tradesmen to the rear," he sniffed, reminding me of the weasel, who I hoped was still concussed.

I flashed my ID. "Official business with the DA."

He was even less impressed at being left to park it.

Widow Escovar met me in the lobby.

"What is it?" she sniffed, dabbing at her eyes.

"I know who killed your husband. I doubt you'll get to see him fry, but we can unmask him, maybe derail his ambition."

She wanted to know who it was, but I told her, "All will be revealed soon."

We joined the crowd gathering to listen to the DA and Daniel Bamford emerged with pious mien to tell us why he was the saviour of our city.

"Since I've become DA, crime has dropped by nearly twenty percent," he expounded.

That was my cue to take to the stage, to his startlement, saying, "But, isn't that due to the deaths of a number of local hoodlums at the hands of *your* goons and your covering-up of several murders, most lately that of Mr Escovar, known as Big Daddy, in order to ensure your acquisition of property likely to soar in value when the interstate is built?”

Now, Daniel Bamford might be the sort who can easily parry a political opponent's points or redirect a reporter's question, but I guess nothing had prepared him for a gumshoe speaking truth to power and he stammered, “But, you should be dead ...”

Had he been a doctor, he might've bluffed his way out of it, but DAs aren't known for their ability to offer a prognosis, save when sending a man to the chair. Even if we couldn't make it stick, his admission and the Widow Escovar's screamed accusations had sunk him in this town.

Still, he might've salvaged his investments and even some credibility and been able to start over somewhere else, but I guess he'd been supping with the Devil with too short a spoon for too long.

He pulled out a gun and shrieked, “I'll kill you!”

Well, you can't get better proof of attempted murder than that.

The bastard shot me.

I shot him back.

Unlike him, I'm a good shot, and tonight, I wasn't aiming at a knee. He went down like the value of shares back in '29, two slugs in his chest, while I merely *sagged*, a bullet lodged in my shoulder.

Sure, I wouldn't be practising my golf swing or playing the violin for a while, but I wasn't dead, and that's what counts at the end of the day in this business.

Thanks to his very-public threat, there could be no doubt I'd shot in self-defence. Even Delgardo would be able to see the truth.

With the DA dead, I wouldn't have to worry about his prosecution and the investigation would discover that all the land he'd bought was held by dead men. Probably some very undeserving relatives, likely every bit as lousy as the dead hoods, would be inheriting some very valuable real estate.

As for me, I'd be receiving a very nice pay-out from the Widow Escovar, even after my hospital fees, so, I guess, we'd all be happy at the outcome.

In fact, the grateful woman proved an attentive nurse, making my recovery swift and sure, and its aftermath pleasant, as she saw to it that I was amply rewarded for avenging her husband.

I can't say whether the interstate will be a good thing for our fair city or not, but, for me, personally, I can say the outcome has been very fine. Very fine, indeed.

BEAUTY KILLS THE BEAST

Marie Anderson

Fairy tales hardly ever come true for quiet girls. But Floria had at last found her Prince Charming. Her quiet days were over. It was time to make things happen. First she had to dispatch Baboon. Her husband. Her rich, old, beastly husband.

"Ouch! God Bless America!" Floria yelled as she ripped off the bandage. There was no one to hear her. She was alone in her dressing room. But being loud felt liberating even though yelling did nothing to lessen the pain. The patch of skin where he'd bitten her neck still burned like a vexatious cold sore. She'd slathered it last night with antibiotic cream and Vitamin E ointment. She touched it now, Baboon's bite mark an ugly tattoo on her otherwise creamy skin.

Well, she wouldn't hide it under a fresh bandage. A bandage would never mesh with the look of sophistication she would achieve tonight. And forget concealing the wound under makeup. He'd sniff the scent, lick it off, he would. He liked marking her, branding her like a rancher brands cows and horses.

She shuddered. That's what she'd felt like married to the Baboon these past 13 months: living meat for Baboon to lick and bite and brand.

Floria draped her mother-in-law's pearls around her neck. The pearls covered part of the wound. That would help. The old crone had given the pearls to Floria for her 25th birthday last month. Lent them actually. The pearls wouldn't really belong to Floria until the crone joined Baboon's father on the fireplace mantle.

There was plenty of room left for the crone in the Tiffany crystal bottles that held the ashes of the late, great, Bruce Wilhelmy II, oil and lumber magnate.

Baboon too.

Floria would make that happen. Baboon first. Tonight.

Floria sat at her makeup table. She smiled at Dit-Dit. Her little bunny sat atop her jewelry box. The pink and white stuffed bunny was the only thing she had left from her life in Colombia.

She cradled it now in the palm of her hand and pressed the bunny's belly the way her grandfather had shown her so many years ago. She pressed in different spots until the bunny squeaked. Its little mouth opened, just wide enough for her finger to squeeze through and remove a slender vial. A milky liquid filled the vial.

Batrachotoxin. Reformulated by her grandfather in his lab in Colombia to be effective orally. Harvested from the beautiful golden arrow frogs he'd caught along the western slopes of the Andes. When she'd had to be smuggled to the States as a frightened 16-year-old to escape her grandfather's enemies, he'd given her the bunny, shown her how to remove the vial he'd hidden inside.

"Floria," he'd said, "this substance is released by the tiny golden frogs in response to agitation, pain, or external threat from predators. It is for you to use like the golden frog. It is like a magic potion that will vanquish your enemies, or, God forbid, take you yourself beyond their reach."

Her grandfather. Her only family. The last time she saw him, she was a sobbing 16-year-old girl, peering at him through the back window of a speeding car. He was standing in front of the only home she'd ever known, waving at her and crying, his final words to her seared in her brain.

"There is enough in your little vial to kill one thousand men."

One thousand men. Tonight she only needed enough for one.

She returned Dit-Dit to its perch atop her jewelry box. She tucked the vial inside her bra cup. Then she slid her new gown over her head.

She studied herself in the full-length mirror. The gown was so light it felt as though she were wearing nothing at all. Her first Vera Wang, size two, $6,000. Way over her monthly allowance. When the charge appeared on their next credit card statement, Baboon would die of a heart attack.

Hopefully.

But with any luck, any guts, long before the next credit card statement, he'd be gone: ashed and stashed inside the crystal Tiffany bottle on their fireplace mantle.

She twirled in front of the mirror, slim as a candy cane, the dress so red, her skin so white except for the nasty red bite mark on her neck. She wondered how long she had before her pregnancy started to show.

She'd probably never wear this gown after tonight, thank God. She didn't like red. It was a loud color, made her feel like she was on fire. But Baboon liked her in red. She'd been wearing a plunging red top when they'd met 17 months ago at the Vegas casino where she'd worked bringing free drinks to the high rollers at the dice tables. He flirted aggressively with all the cocktail girls, but her quiet smiles and lowered eyes presented a challenge to him. "This one," he announced to the dice table, "is probably loud where it counts! And I aim to find out!"

But she didn't let him try to find out until their wedding night.

She patted her flat stomach. She'd done the test with a drugstore kit last week. The stick had turned blue. Pregnant.

At last.

Her stomach tickled as she envisioned the look on her lover's face when she told him tonight. Tonight, surely tonight, she'd manage to tell him the exciting news. Oh, how she missed him. Twenty-nine days since their last tryst. Twenty-nine days she'd attended morning Mass in the grand cathedral four blocks from the grand Wilhelmy mansion. Twenty-nine days she'd waited for Hulio T's agent to slip into a nearby pew. Her signal that Hulio T would be waiting for her in the florist van parked down the block from the cathedral.

Twenty-nine days where he hadn't even let her know he was out of town.

He had some explaining to do. She'd seen the recent photos in *Star Magazine*, Hulio partying at a Vegas nightclub, a curvy beautiful redhead at his side.

She'd see him tonight. Tonight he'd be crooning the crowd of rich, lacquered guests at the fundraising gala at the City Zoo. She and Baboon, of course, would have a front table. Hulio would see her, aflame in her red gown, a fiery rose among plastic plants. He'd fall in love with her all over again.

"Floria!" Baboon's quavery old-man's voice shattered her daydream. He pawed her locked door.

"Almost ready, Bruce!" she shouted.

"I'll be awaiting downstairs, little filly," he said. "Get that sweet little rump moving."

She listened while he clomped away. Then she lipsticked her mouth, slipped into her red glitter sandals, and hip-swiveled down the curving stairs.

Baboon stood in their foyer, watching her, or rather watching her body. His silver mane of hair glistened under the blaze from the overhead chandelier. The chandelier hung 20 feet over his head, its crystals sharp and glistening, quivering ever so gently, ready to plunge and shatter the enemy below.

If only.

Floria stretched her lips into a smile and wiggled to his side. As always, she felt herself shrink next to him. He was triple her weight, double her width, though only a head taller than she.

She could tell that he'd had two martinis too many. His face glistened with sweat. His cheeks burned red, as red as his saggy butt cheeks had been last night after she'd spanked him. Forever he'd had her swat him until her arm ached. When at last he was snoring wetly into his pillow, she'd rushed to their bathroom and thrown up the entire meal Chef Luis had prepared for their dinner: the beef tenderloin in cherry sauce, the rosemary-roasted new potatoes. The crème brulée too.

The memory now triggered a sour burp. Baboon heard it, his hearing acute despite the white hair clogging his pendulous ears.

"Sick!" he squealed. "My little bunny burping. She needum her papa to pat her wittle back!" His moist, hairy paw gripped her bare shoulder.

"Bruce! We have to go!" She swallowed back another burp.

"Ah, silly filly. You look goody enough to eat!"

She froze. The houseman, standing by their front door, studied his shiny black shoes. Baboon lowered his silver-maned head, bared his yellowing choppers, and nipped her neck.

"Ouch!" She slapped his cheek.

"You feisty filly!" He bit her neck again.

"Bruce!" With a huge act of will, she lowered her voice into the breathy whispers he loved. "Brucie, not now. Later. I promise."

"Ahh," he nasaled. She smiled so hard her face hurt. How, she wondered, could one syllable be so full of nose.

"I shall hold you to that, filly," he said.

"Brucie!" The crone's screechy voice made Floria's heart jump. The old woman tottered down the stairs. "Let me have a look-see at my handsome boy!"

She shuffled close to Baboon, stepping on Floria's toes. Liver-spotted hands fussed with his bow tie and cummerbund. "Don't stay out too late now," she said. "You have your board meeting tomorrow morning."

"You bet, Mama," he said.

She looked at Floria, her watery brown eyes traveling up and down Floria's body.

"Make sure this one gets watered and fed tonight," she said to Baboon. "Life can't bloom in sterile barren deserts."

"You bet, Mama," he said.

The crone fingered the pearls around Floria's neck.

"My pearls look good," she said to Floria, "but you better see a doctor for that rash." She pointed at the wound of Floria's neck.

"You bet, Mama," she murmured.

Their houseman opened the door, and Floria and Baboon stepped out. The cool spring air bit her bare toes. She slipped into the back seat of their Cadillac Escalade. Baboon huffed and puffed and stuffed himself next to her. The TV was turned to *Wheel of Fortune*, his favorite show. The chauffeur looked at Floria, his eyes soft with sadness as he raised the opaque glass.

Somehow they made it to the zoo without Floria enduring any more bites or any wardrobe malfunctions.

Thank you *Wheel of Fortune*.

As soon as they stepped into the huge tent, cameras flashed. Other guests swarmed. Baboon was rich and powerful, a tempting target for ruthless kidnappers or fanatics who considered it a capital offense to rape the earth for oil and lumber.

In her dreams.

After dessert, the lights dimmed. The crowd hushed. The only sound Floria could hear was Baboon's phlegmy breathing. A spotlight stabbed the center of the stage right in front of Floria's table. And there stood Hulio T. Tall, dark, handsome. His black curls shiny and wet, looking to Floria like a glorious god just emerged from a waterfall. His blue eyes looked everywhere but at her. He began to sing, and Floria felt as though warm butter was soothing her skin.

After a few songs, Floria felt Baboon's paw on her thigh. His extraordinarily long thumb began to poke into the fabric of her silk gown. Though she couldn't see it in the dark, she knew his thumb nail was thick and fungus-yellow.

She pushed his paw away.

"Huh," he grunted. Floria could feel his scowl. His rancid breath shivered her ear. "You need a drink," he said. "You haven't drunk a bit all night. Drink up now. Get loose."

Floria bit her lip. She could feel the vial against her breast, tucked in her bra. Soon was the time she'd have to slip it out and pour a few drops into his glass of red wine. She'd been practicing in the dark in her dressing room at night, using a tiny vial she'd bought at a craft store that she'd filled with water.

Harder to do it surrounded by so many, but if an autopsy were done and the toxin detected, the suspicion would be far less strong on her. Waiters, bartenders, other guests, hundreds would have had opportunity.

"I did it my way!" Hulio T sang. The crowd roared. Lights flickered on. Intermission time.

Baboon's broad nostrils flared. He blinked his watery brown eyes. He held her full glass of red wine under her nose. "A toast, Floria," he shouted. "To another successful fundraiser for our great city's world class zoo."

"Bruce," she whispered. Others at their table were staring at them, their mouths slightly open, the men flushed and silent, the women's eyes glittering, their pupils large and predatory.

"Bruce," she whispered again, pursing her lips against his hairy ear. "I can't. No more alcohol for me for nine months. You're going to be a papa."

Baboon gasped. He pushed her wine glass far away from her. He fell back in his chair. She could sense the joy throttling his muscles, the heat sizzling his veins. His crepey neck pulsed, as though his heart were doing jumping jacks.

"Mother," he choked. "I've gotta tell Mother!" He pawed at the pockets of his tux. "Where's my phone? Anyone? Anyone got a phone I can use?"

If you'd let me carry a purse I'd have my own phone, Floria thought.

"Oh, this is … this is … when, darling? Oh my fertile little turtle! When will I be a proud papa?"

Floria smiled. This hadn't been her plan. The words had just tumbled out. He hadn't been this happy with her since their wedding night. She was wife number six. None had produced an heir for him. Certainly it wasn't impossible that this child was his. But she knew, she *knew,* that her baby would never grow a big nostrilly nose or yellow teeth or pendulous ears.

"Everyone!" He lurched to his feet. "Great news! I've just found out I'm going to be a father!"

People cheered. Cameras flashed. Glasses rose high in a toast. Baboon swayed and toppled, gripping the tablecloth as he fell, so that everything fell with him. Plates, drinks, cutlery, the full coffee pot, and the centerpiece of fragrant red roses.

She hadn't needed the magic potion after all.

A massive heart attack had done the job.

Baboon's ashes were safely sealed in three new Tiffany crystal bottles on Floria's fireplace mantle. Her mother-in-law was safely sedated in one of the upstairs bedroom suites. Hulio T sat next to her on the sofa, staring into the fire crackling in the fireplace.

At last, he looked at her.

"Sorry, babe," he said. "But I need the do-re-mi more than I need a woman, you know what I'm saying?"

"I thought you loved me," she said.

He nodded. "I do, babe. But the Hulio T is a free spirit. If you love him, you gotta let him fly. So share the cash and you'll never have to worry about me demanding a paternity test. We'll both win. You'll be rich the rest of your life. My little Hulio or Hulia in there"—he patted her still flat belly—"is your meal ticket, you play your cards right. It blasts your pre-nup into little bits no legal lawyer gonna ever glue back together. You know what I'm saying?"

Floria bit her lower lip so hard she drew blood. Under the terms of her pre-nup, she'd agreed to forfeit everything should Baboon pass and she remarry. But she'd been willing to forfeit wealth for love.

Now she stared into the blue eyes of her tarnished Prince Charming and sighed. "How can I trust you not to come back sometime, demanding more?"

"Babe, my word is gold."

She remembered how he'd said he'd love her, forever and ever. She'd be his princess. He'd be her prince.

"You've got that little gambling passion, Hulio. What about that? How can I trust that?"

"Babe, you gotta believe me when I say that's the past. The dice used to suck my money like a swamp sucks dead bodies. I can't argue with the past. But I gotta new system, can't lose. It's sure-fire. The dice tables gonna bow down to the Hulio T, babe. They gonna spit those green and black chips into my tray like a tweaker upchucking his Big Macs."

Floria stared at him. He stared right back, the heat from his blue, blue eyes burning a hole in her heart.

"Well, tell me your sure-fire system," she said.

And so he did, describing an elaborate pattern of laying odds, placing sixes and eights, and making come bets after the shooter had made a certain number of points.

"OK," she said when at last he paused. "I'll need a few days to get the cash. But let's seal the deal now with a drink."

She returned a short time later with two flutes filled with champagne. She just wet her lips while he downed his in three swallows.

Nothing happened. She watched in dismay as Hulio T drove away.

But later, she watched the YouTube video. Hulio T at a nightclub only minutes from her mansion, toppling off his chair, saliva drooling from twitching lips, body convulsing on the floor, gasping, while horrified onlookers screamed for help.

He died on the way to the hospital.

Of course an autopsy was done. And a tox screen. She waited to hear the results. She'd only put a tiny amount in his drink. A bit of liquid no more than a few grains of salt. Would the tox screen detect it?

It did not.

Just as her grandfather had promised.

The tox screen had found the usual villains in Hulio T's system: alcohol, coke, Adderall, marijuana. Death from cardiac arrest was the finding, likely triggered by a lethal combination of drugs and alcohol.

Magic potion indeed.

Little Bruce Wilhelmy IV was born on Christmas Day. Eyes blue. Hair soft, fuzzy, and black. Floria took to calling him Baby Boon-Boon when she sang lullabies, and soon everyone, even the adoring old crone, was calling the little guy Boon.

"He's our blessing," the crone said at Boon's baptism. "Our gift. Our precious boon from God."

And everyone not dead lived happily ever after.

THE CORPSE THAT COULDN'T LIE

A You-Solve-It by Martin Hill Ortiz

Upon entering the Jacobs Manor's library, Inspector Crispen Dunsworthy blanched: he could hardly imagine a more chaotic nor more grisly scene. Furniture was slashed. The shards of a heavy glass ashtray were strewn across the chimney hearth. The body of seventy-year-old Dr. Hiram Jacobs lay on his back, a butcher's knife protruding from his chest. Zig-zags of blood spattered the floor and puddled next to the body. The doctor had not merely been killed, he had been mutilated: someone had cut off his lips.

A cold draft whistled down the chimney flue.

"The mansion has security cameras," Seargent Biddles informed him, "but they are poorly maintained and most are out of order. Only one is of use. It looks down the hallway leading up to the entrance to the library."

"And what does it show?" the inspector asked, stroking his jaw: his tooth ached.

"Only three people have passed down the corridor in the last hour," Biddles said. "I have assembled them and they are standing here before you." A stooped elderly man, a youth of about twenty, and a pouting woman in her mid-thirties. "The first to arrive was ..."

"Me," the young man said. "I am Paulie Jacobs." He wore a blond suede jacket over a white shirt and a loosely fitted dress tie. His feet were bare. "The victim is my father."

"According to the video," Biddles said, "Paulie passed down the hall in the direction of the library at 8:23 p.m. He was seen again leaving at 8:35."

"We had a talk," Paulie said. "My father and I. He was alive when I left."

The inspector pressed close to the young man. He smelled liquor on his breath. "And what did you discuss?"

"His will. My father cut me out. He is leaving everything to Miss Wanamaker. He promised me the house. His lying, lying lips. I'm afraid I was the one who threw the ashtray. I missed."

"I am Polly Wanamaker," the woman said. "I am, I mean, I was Dr. Jacobs's personal secretary."

"Very personal," Paulie added.

Seargent Biddles flipped a page in his notebook. He said, "Going by the time-stamp, Miss Wanamaker passed down the corridor going to the library at 8:43 and stayed for seven minutes."

Dunsworthy noted that this woman didn't seem particularly broken up by the doctor's death. She appeared to be dressed for an evening out. She wore a black sequined dress that squeezed her more tightly than would a python. Her puckered lips conveyed an impish smile.

"And was Dr. Jacobs alive when you arrived?" the inspector asked.

"And when you left?" Paulie added.

"I didn't enter the library," Polly said. "I suppose you can't see this on the camera, but I continued on down the hall to a corner closet to retrieve my favorite hat."

The inspector arched his eyebrows. "It took you seven minutes to collect a hat?"

"I couldn't decide which one was my favorite. Eventually, I gave up. You will see in the tape that I returned down the hall with no hat at all, proving my story."

Paulie Jacobs rolled his eyes.

"Besides," Polly continued, "Jakie left me everything. I have no motive."

"Unless you couldn't wait to inherit," Paulie pointed out.

Polly laughed, a tiny chirp. "I rather enjoyed his lips," she said.

Biddles again consulted his notes, "Finally, Dr. Oliver Stitz, Dr. Jacobs's long-time partner in their medical practice. He headed down the corridor, four minutes past nine. After half a minute, he returned, and in a hurry."

Like the victim, Oliver was about seventy. He was stooped and impeccably dressed in an Italian suit with shoes so polished that they gleamed. "Half a minute. I certainly didn't have time for the murder and all this chaos."

"Why did you leave so quickly?" the inspector asked.

"I had to call for an ambulance," the doctor said. "I'd left my cellular in my jacket pocket, downstairs on the coat rack."

"An ambulance? So Jacobs was alive when you came upon him?" Biddles asked.

"Yes," Dr. Stitz said. "And, what's more he whispered to me the name of the murderer."

All those listening hushed in anticipation.

"My good friend said, 'Pah-lee did it.' "

"Liar!" Paulie said, adding a dismissive sniff.

"Wait," Polly said, "did he say Paulie or Polly?"

Dr. Stitz shrugged.

"Oh, come on," Paulie said. "Do you really believe my father so conveniently spoke his killer's name with his last breaths?"

"Yes, I do," Inspector Dunsworthy declared. "Dr. Jacobs did identify his killer and gave enough information to sort out exactly who it was."

Who did it?

Solution in next month's issue ...

SOLUTION TO JULY'S YOU-SOLVE-IT

The Green Burglar by John H. Dromey

"Photos of one of your crime scenes were shared with every member of the department. Apparently, you transferred coal dust or wood ash, or whatever, from a fireplace to the soles of your sneakers before walking across a pale, low pile carpet. The lacerations of your footwear were clearly defined in the trace evidence. Later, Officers Bishop and Cody recognized those unique patterns in your snowy footprints."

Syd had no choice but to trade his green lifestyle for an orange jumpsuit.

MysteryMagazine.ca